"Will you come live here as my wife?" Jonas asked

Lucy looked at him thoughtfully. "Would that include sharing your bed?"

His eyes mocked her. "Is the prospect so very daunting?"

"Since I haven't given it any thought," she lied, "I don't really know. But I need to have the terms all spelled out for me before I agree. *If* I agree, that is."

Lucy paused, then said, "Because if my son doesn't like the idea, then the whole thing is off."

A pulse throbbed at the corner of Jonas's mouth. "And if he approves, will you consent?"

Lucy was afraid to answer. The way she felt about this man was baffling. Was it really true what they said about love being the reverse side of hate?

CATHERINE GEORGE was born in Wales, and following her marriage to an engineer, lived eight years in Brazil at a gold mine site, an experience she would later draw upon for her books. It was not until she and her husband returned to England and bought a village post office and general store that she submitted her first book at her husband's encouragement. Now her husband helps manage their household so that Catherine can devote more time to her writing. They have two children, a daughter and a son, who share their mother's love of language and writing.

Books by Catherine George

HARLEQUIN PRESENTS

800—PRODIGAL SISTER
858—INNOCENT PAWN
873—SILENT CRESCENDO
992—THE MARRIAGE BED
1016—LOVE LIES SLEEPING
1065—TOUCH ME IN THE MORNING

HARLEQUIN ROMANCE

2535—RELUCTANT PARAGON
2571—DREAM OF MIDSUMMER
2720—DESIRABLE PROPERTY
2822—THE FOLLY OF LOVING
2924—MAN OF IRON
2942—THIS TIME ROUND

Don't miss any of our special offers. Write to us at the following address for information on our newest releases.

Harlequin Reader Service
901 Fuhrmann Blvd., P.O. Box 1397, Buffalo, NY 14240
Canadian address: P.O. Box 603,
Fort Erie, Ont. L2A 5X3

CATHERINE GEORGE

villain of the piece

Harlequin Books

TORONTO • NEW YORK • LONDON
AMSTERDAM • PARIS • SYDNEY • HAMBURG
STOCKHOLM • ATHENS • TOKYO • MILAN

Harlequin Presents first edition March 1989
ISBN 0-373-11152-5

Original hardcover edition published in 1988
by Mills & Boon Limited

CHAPTER ONE

TO MOST of its inhabitants, the principal charm of Abbotsbridge was its lack of proximity to any motorway. Bustling and friendly, not yet taken over by the developer, the small market town lay in a hollow surrounded by countryside straight from a Constable painting, and as a rule Lucy Drummond was happy to call it home. But tonight for once, she thought, sighing, she would have appreciated major, brightly lit roads. The heavy snowfall of the past week had begun a slow thaw earlier, making Lucy's outward journey relatively straightforward, but, with nightfall, temperatures were down to freezing again, glazing the road with icy patches. Worst of all, fog had reduced visibility to a few yards.

Lucy gave a vote of thanks to the inventor of the cat's eyes reflecting her headlights in the centre of the road, and eased the tension between her shoulderblades as she peered through the windscreen. She drove at a snail's pace, worried about missing the sign for Abbotsbridge. Luckily there was very little traffic on the road. Sensible people had stayed indoors on this freezing Sunday evening, and Lucy wished she could have done the same. She gritted her teeth as the fog thickened, doing her best to be philosophical. Such intense concentration was a boon in one way. It left no room for depression about parting with Tom,

which was an occurrence she never got used to. The
swift goodbye kiss, the lonely journey back . . . She
blinked hard, straining to see through the
blanketing whiteness, then gave a sigh of relief as
the sign she was looking for showed dimly through
the fog. At last! Feeling better at once, she turned
off on the road for Abbotsbridge.

Lucy's relief was short-lived. She stiffened,
slamming on the brakes. No more friendly little
glow-worms in the middle of the road. She'd taken
the wrong turning. Her heart sank as she
recognised the private road leading to Abbot's
Wood, just about the last house in the world she
had any desire to be even near.

Instead of raging at herself, Lucy saved her
energies for the task of navigating the big old estate
car along a road which was lined either side by deep
ditches, or had been in the days when she used to
cycle along it regularly. Her lips tightened. One
small comfort was that no one was likely to be
about to accuse her of trespassing, least of all
Jonas Woodbridge, the owner of Abbot's Wood.
The town's most celebrated citizen was invariably
up the Limpopo or the Hindu Kush or wherever,
gathering material for his books, and rarely graced
Abbotsbridge with his presence these days. Lucy
gasped, paying at once for her lapse of concentration as the car went into a skid on a patch of ice.
Somehow she managed to avoid braking sharply,
but her heart was thudding as she drove on with
more caution, envying people who lived in cities
with bright lights and no fog. Oh, God, how she
wished she were home!

The fog thinned a little as she passed the gates of
Abbot's Wood, and Lucy drove with more confi-

dence as she left them behind. Her spirits rose. Another mile or so and she would be back on Abbotsbridge road. The thought had barely crossed her mind when she hit a sudden blank wall of fog and braked instinctively. The wheels slewed across a sheet of ice and she screamed as the car careered off the road into the snow-filled ditch, coming to rest at a drunken angle.

After an interval of reassuring herself she was in one piece, Lucy fumbled with her seat-belt, her shaking fingers making heavy work of releasing the catch as she twisted to compensate for the tilt of the car. Miraculously, one headlight was still working, and by its beam Lucy managed to extricate herself and her belongings and heave herself out on to the road. Teeth chattering, she scrabbled in her bag for the small torch she always carried and shone it on the car. The extent of the damage was difficult to estimate in the dim light, but one thing was glaringly apparent. Without a tow-truck to haul it out of the ditch, the car would have to stay put. She had no option but to walk the remaining couple of miles home.

After a struggle to turn off the headlight, Lucy locked the car and began to trudge along the road. It was narrow, with high, snow-covered hedgerows either side, and with only torchlight for illumination it looked altogether too eerie for comfort. She turned up her collar and walked as fast as she could through the eddying fog, which trailed chilly wisps of itself against her face like ghostly fingers . . . 'And that's enough of that, Lucy Drummond,' she said aloud, consoling herself with the thought that the adventure would at least be something to write to Tom about in her twice-weekly letter.

Lucy was euphoric when she reached the Abbotsbridge road. There was still a mile or so to go, but once off Woodbridge land she felt a lot better, and quickened her pace. Half an hour later she turned up the lane which led to Holly Lodge, almost weak at the knees with relief. Home! The peeling white gates stood open, as always, and beyond them, like a scarecrow mocking her through the fog, loomed the hated For Sale sign. Lucy frowned as she reached the front door. Odd. The house was in darkness. And she was quite certain she'd left lights on, because Tom had reminded her about it. She shone the beam on the door and unlocked it, opening it warily. No intruder rushed out to mug her; instead there was just darkness and a very ominous dripping sound.

With foreboding, Lucy turned on the light switch in the hall. Nothing happened. In horror, she shone the torch on great sodden patches of the hall carpet, at water still dripping fitfully through the ceiling above, then she jumped yards as a loud, rending noise came from upstairs. Lucy sprinted up to the landing, appalled as she shone her feeble light on the floor at mounds of plaster that had once been the ceiling. With a groan she dashed through the rest of the rooms, but to her relief the main damage appeared to be in the hall and on the upper landing. The little torch began to flicker, and she flew down to the hall closet for the big one kept there for power-cuts, then went into the kitchen to rummage in drawers for candles, saucers, matches. Blast the snow! she thought with venom. Why couldn't it just look pretty, instead of causing accidents and bursting pipes? Especially when the victim was Lucy Drummond.

Once every candle she could lay her hands on was lit, Lucy tried to calm down, think what to do. It was a bit like locking the stable after the horse was gone, but just the same it seemed prudent to turn off the stopcock in the cupboard in the hall. Telephone, next. Ring the plumber, the electrician. To her consternation, her replies came from the wives of the respective gentlemen. They sympathised with her greatly, but their menfolk were already out on similar calls, and had been all day. But her name would be added to the list, they assured her.

Deeply depressed, Lucy waded again through the debris on the upper landing, struck by the thought that not even a cup of tea was forthcoming by way of comfort. Almost simultaneously she heard another ripping, groaning noise and something hit her on the head, and she sat down hard among the rubble with a screech. It was too much. But any desire to cry noisily died an instant death. She stiffened, her mouth drying, as she heard movement in the darkness downstairs. In her panic, she had forgotten to lock the front door. Someone was in the house with her. Rigid with fear, Lucy switched off the heavy rubber torch and got very quietly to her feet. Footsteps sounded on the stairs, and at the very moment that a voice called her name Lucy swung out wildly with the torch and connected with the owner of the voice, screaming her head off, lost to all rational behaviour by this stage, and convinced she was about to be attacked.

There were curses and scuffling about, as hands seized her, and Lucy fought savagely to get free.

then a voice panted in her ear, 'For God's sake,
Lucy, be still; you've almost blinded me!'

Lucy recognised the voice and froze, the mere
sound of it acting like a cold sponge.

The man shook her slighly. 'Are you hurt? Did
someone break in? Are you all *right*, Lucy—*tell*
me!'

She was yanked to her feet and the torch shone
in her face. She blinked like a mole coming out of
its burrow, blinded by the light.

'I'm fine,' she said hoarsely, and shivered. The
man cursed, and touched a finger to her forehead.

'You're cut,' he said tersely. 'Can you walk?'

'Of course I can,' Lucy said irritably, and
suffered herself to be marched downstairs, still
shivering, chilled to the bone. 'What are you doing
here, Joss?' she asked dully, too numb by this time
to feel surprise about anything much.

Jonas Woodbridge stared down at her by the
flickering light of the candles dotted round the
kitchen. 'The door was open. I called, but your
only response was to assault me with that bloody
torch. I know perfectly well I'm *persona non grata*
with you, Lucy, nevertheless I was worried when I
found your car in the ditch near my place.'

Lucy shrugged. 'Sorry to clutter up your private
road.'

His mouth tightened. 'Were you hurt when the
car went over?'

'No, no. I walked home from there.'

'Then why the blood on your forehead?'

'A piece of ceiling just fell on me.'

'A bad case of burst pipes, I take it.'

She nodded despondently, and Joss Woodbridge
looked at her for some time. 'Where's Tom?' he

asked at last.

'He went back this afternoon. I was driving home when I went into the ditch.'

He rubbed his chin, eyeing her curiously. 'Were you coming to see *me*, Lucy?'

She stared at him blankly. 'See *you*? Good lord, no.'

His face hardened. 'Then why were you on my private road?'

'I took the wrong turning in the fog.'

There was another awkward silence, while Lucy willed Joss Woodbridge to take himself off. It was a long time since she'd last seen him, and even longer since they'd spoken to each other. The dim, flickering light played odd tricks with his face, but she knew the angles and hollows of it as well as she knew her own. No bright lights were necessary to see that he was as tall and graceful as ever, with no spare flesh on his broad-shouldered frame. And he was still the most physically beautiful man she had ever seen. A face like a fallen angel, her father had once said. It was a good description. There had always been a subtle difference between Joss and his younger brother, the inseparable companion of Lucy Drummond's girlhood. Simon had been just as handsome, but a sunny, joyous soul, loved by everyone, including Joss. Especially Joss.

'I *said*,' repeated Joss impatiently, 'have you rung a plumber?'

Lucy blinked. 'Oh—yes. And the electrician. No dice. They're already out on calls.'

'I'll get Ted Carter on to it first thing in the morning.'

Lucy had no stomach for help from Joss Woodbridge, not even in the shape of Ted Carter, the very pleasant man who ran the Abbot's Wood estate for him. 'Please don't trouble yourself,' she said stiffly. 'The repairs will get done in time.'

Joss moved swiftly to grasp her shoulders, with the co-ordinated economy that was peculiarly his own. 'And in the meantime, Lucy Drummond, how are you likely to manage without light, heat—even water?' His eyes bored into hers as he shook her slightly. 'Is it still so impossible to accept any help from me? Even after all these years?'

'Yes,' said Lucy flatly.

He dropped his hands and stood back. 'So you still bear the same old grudge, Lucy. Have you never considered your attitude unfair? You know better than anyone in the world that I was off my head with grief when Simon died. I hardly knew what I was saying that day. I swear I never meant to hurt you so deeply.'

'Heaven protect me, then,' she said delicately, 'if you ever do.' She turned away. 'Now I'd better let you go, and start on some telephoning. I think I know where I can beg a bed for the night, since home isn't exactly sweet *pro tem*.'

Joss seemed about to say something, then shrugged and moved to the door. 'Very well, Lucy. But if you need anything——'

'I shan't.' Not from you, she added silently, and felt a flare of satisfaction as she saw him read her mind.

'Goodnight, Lucy.' Joss went out without looking at her, leaving her alone by the light of the guttering candles.

Swiftly Lucy dialled the number of her friend, Perdy Roche. Perdy threw exquisite pots in her tiny riverside studio on the outskirts of Abbotsbridge, but to Lucy's dismay her friend's dulcet tones on the answering machine were the only response, which meant Perdy's weekend with her new man was being extended to Monday. This narrowed the choices down to staying the night at home in the dark, which Lucy really didn't fancy at all, or a long, cold hike into town to camp out in the flat above the shop.

'This,' she said aloud, 'is quite definitely not my day.'

'No room at the inn?' asked Joss, frightening the life out of her as he reappeared through the gloom.

Lucy glared at him. 'Is eavesdropping a hobby of yours?'

'No.' He stood just inside the door, hands in pockets. 'But, purely for my own peace of mind, I'd prefer to know you're somewhere safe before I go home. My motives were pure, I promise. I thought I'd wait to give you a lift to wherever you want to go.'

Lucy was tempted to say she'd rather walk barefoot, but pocketed her pride. 'In that case, since Perdy Roche isn't at home, perhaps you wouldn't mind running me into town. I'll camp out at the shop tonight.'

'On a chaise-longue in the window?'

'No.' Lucy hung on to her temper with an effort. 'In the flat above.'

His eyebrows rose. 'Is it furnished, then?'

'Not much. But it has electricity, so it beats this place hands down for the moment.'

He gave a brief nod. 'Very well. I'll wait in the car while you collect your things.'

'Thank you.' Lucy flew upstairs, torch in hand, threw some clothes into an overnight bag, then as

an afterthought collected a few basic foodstuffs
from the kitchen and locked up the house. The
familiar Abbot's Wood Land Rover was waiting at
the gate, with Joss Woodbridge leaning against it,
smoking. He threw the cigar away as Lucy
appeared, and took her bag before installing her in
the passenger seat with impersonal courtesy. As
they drove away, Lucy frowned.

'By the way, how did you come to see my car,
Joss? It was quite a way from your place.'

'I was on my way home from Ted Carter's when
I saw the car in the ditch. Naturally I stopped to see
if anyone was inside in need of help, saw the
number plate and realised it was yours.'

'How did you know it was mine?' she asked
curiously.

'I knew.' He glanced sideways at her. 'It's quite
easy to keep track of you, Lucy.'

She stared stonily through the windscreen at the
fog. 'Yes, of course. Lucy Drummond's a
household name in Abbotsbridge.'

'In the kindest possible way, surely?'

'Oh, absolutely. Everyone's *very* kind to me.
Always.' She sighed. 'Sometimes it's suffocating. I
long for the anonymity of a big city—but it's out of
the question. Tom loves it here, and it's where I
make my living, so I stay put. Probably it'll be on
my epitaph. "Lucy Drummond, born, bred and
died in Abbotsbridge".'

The bitterness in her tone was by no means lost
on her companion, Lucy knew, but he drove on in
silence until she exclaimed and leaned forward to
peer at the road. 'Joss—you've missed the
turning.'

'So I have,' He sounded unsurprised. 'In that

case, I might as well take you back to Abbot's Wood.'

'What?' Lucy twisted to look at him, appalled, but Joss drove on unmoved. 'Please, Joss. You must know how unsuitable this is.'

He shook his head. 'Why? To me, it seems the height of folly to lie on the floor over your shop when several empty bedrooms are going begging at my place. And if you're worried about the proprieties, the Bensons are still with me under my roof. Your reputation will be perfectly safe.'

Lucy's chin lifted. 'All very funny to you, no doubt, but it's a very important consideration to—to someone like me.'

'Yes, Lucy,' he agreed quietly. 'I'm sure it is. But just the same I insist you stay the night in comfort—and safety.'

Lucy subsided, aware that she ought to feel offended by his high-handedness, but suddenly too tired to put up any more opposition. She had no yen for a solitary night on a hard floor, if she were honest. If the offer of a bed had come from anyone but Jonas Woodbridge she'd have jumped at it, she knew. It was only common sense to take him up on it just for one night. There were so many unsolved problems in her life at the moment that it was good to have someone take over for her, if only for an hour or two, giving her breathing space from the worries that seemed to multiply by the day.

'Do I take your silence as consent?' Joss enquired.

'Yes. All right. Thank you.' Lucy rubbed at her eyes. 'I expect it's only because you've caught me at a bad time, but to be honest I don't seem to have enough energy to argue.'

'Which must be a one-off!' Joss laughed shortly, and swung the Land Rover up the long curve of the driveway leading to Abbot's Wood. Lucy slid down from the vehicle when it stopped, suddenly tense as she looked up at the house she had once known so well. Joss took her by the arm and led her to the wide door. Soft yellow light shone from the graceful fanlight above it, and from the long windows either side, warm and welcoming through the swirling fog, but Lucy shivered.

'Cold?' Joss opened the door and ushered her into the hall.

Not cold, thought Lucy. Haunted. She stood just inside the door, looking across the shining expanse of polished wood floor, at the familiar Persian rugs, the staircase with the portraits on the panelled wall, and she swallowed hard on the lump in her throat. It all looked so much the same, it was hard to believe Simon wouldn't come running down the stairs at any minute, grinning all over his handsome face. Joss seemed to sense her reaction and moved towards her, hand outstretched, but she shrank away and the hand dropped.

'I'll get Mrs Benson,' he said quietly, and went through a door at the back of the hall.

Alone, Lucy looked down at herself disparagingly. Her sweater was newish, but her tweed skirt and fleece-lined suede boots had been in service for some time, and she had a fair idea her face and hair looked a mess. In all the panic in the damp and darkness at Holly Lodge, her appearance had been the last thing on her mind. But here, in this beautifully-proportioned hall, with its stone fireplace and Florentine mirrors, she felt bedraggled and depressed.

Joss's return, in company with Mrs Benson, brought her out of her preoccupation with a start.

The neat, grey-haired woman beamed in welcome. 'Lucy—how very nice to see you. Such a nasty night! Mr Jonas says you've had some bother at home, my dear.'

Lucy smiled in wry agreement, and furnished the depressing details as she was shepherded upstairs to a wonderfully warm guest-room. Mr Jonas would be waiting in the study, Mrs Benson told her, as she left Lucy to perform a few rapid repairs. After a vigorous wash in the pretty bathroom, followed by an energetic attack on her curly, dark hair with a brush, some instinct prompted Lucy to add a touch of colour to her eyes and cheeks. Armour? she asked her reflection, then went quietly downstairs to the study door and knocked.

Joss welcomed her into the room she'd never been inside before. Applewood logs from the orchard behind the house crackled in the big open fireplace, and Lucy held out her hands to the blaze, looking with professional interest at the Georgian knee-hole desk, the plain, leather-topped table piled with papers and books, surprised to see a word-processor on a workmanlike pine desk beside it. The modern items looked alien in the book-lined room.

'So this is where you write,' she said, and turned to look at Joss Woodbridge full in the face for the first time in the light. He returned the look with interest, his eyes travelling over her impersonally from the rubbed toes of her boots up over the brown tweed skirt and pink sweater to her face. Joss's face was burnt dark by some fierce foreign sun, and Lucy felt an unexpected pang as she saw the lines fanning palely at the corners of his slate-blue eyes. He was so like Simon, she thought with pain; the same thick brown hair, but the gold glints she remembered so clearly were silver now, adding a final touch of maturity to a face that had aged almost overnight all those years before. Once upon a time Joss Woodbridge had been more beautiful than any man had a right to be. Now he was different. There was a world-weary look in those slanting blue eyes, and a hard set to the beautifully-cut mouth; not that either factor, she thought drily, was likely to detract one iota from the attraction Jonas Woodbridge possessed for the female of the species.

Lucy allowed Joss to settle her by the fire, near a small table set with a tea-tray and a silver platter of delicately cut sandwiches.

'I thought you might have missed dinner in all the excitement,' he said, then shrugged, grinning. 'Besides, Mrs Benson was convinced you'd be starving. She said you were always hungry in the old days.'

'And had the figure to prove it,' said Lucy wryly. 'But please thank Mrs Benson. It can't be much fun having unexpected guests arrive late at night.'

'It happens too rarely to present a problem.' He eyed her closely. 'Aren't you a bit on the thin side, Lucy? You were a lot rounder once.'

'I was a lot of things once that now I'm not. Who isn't?' Lucy poured herself some tea and changed the subject. 'Where have you been recently then, Joss? Somewhere hot, by the look of you.'

'Fiji.'

'And now you're home to write a book about it?'

'Yes. For a few months or so. Then I've been commissioned to do a book on Brazil. The effect of the erosion of their rain-forest on an Indian tribe in the Amazon basin.' Joss lounged in a chair opposite, staring absently into the fire.

'I saw a programme you did on television. Mauritius, was it?'

'Did you enjoy it?'

'Very much.' Lucy sighed. 'But programmes like that depress me sometimes. Faraway places with strange-sounding names tend to make me restless.'

Joss turned to look at her. 'Don't you ever go on holiday, Lucy?'

'When I can manage it. But only in this country. Nowhere exotic.'

There was a pause, then Joss said quietly, 'I was sorry to hear about your father, Lucy. I liked him enormously. You must miss him very much.'

Lucy's dark eyes shadowed. 'He went in the way he'd have chosen, you know, after a reunion dinner with old RAF cronies, reliving the past. He came home, went to bed—and never woke up. Tom and I were flattened. It was so unexpected. I mean—Dad wasn't that old. Only sixty-eight. And always such a live wire.'

'Is that why you've put the lodge up for sale?

'Partly. There are other reasons, too.' Lucy changed the subject firmly, casting about her for inspiration. 'I'm surprised to see a word-processor,' she said brightly. 'Somehow I'd always pictured you with a gold pen, writing at a desk something like the Georgian one over there. Not that I'd ever seen this room, of course. You wouldn't let Simon and me near it. You kept it locked.'

'Which means I was wise about one thing, at least. The rest of the time I didn't do very well at all with Simon, did I? Nor with you, Lucy.' The long blue eyes met hers with unmistakable meaning, and between one instant and the next the atmosphere changed, electric with things unsaid, and Lucy stared back, mesmerised, unable to look away. Colour washed her face, then receded, leaving her deathly pale as memories flooded back. From the look on his face it was all too evident that Joss was remembering the same thing; that day in another time, another life, when they had found themselves so unexpectedly alone together in this very house. But then it had been hot, humid summertime, and she had been young and helplessly, hopelessly in love . . . Lucy drew in a long, shaking breath and Joss sprang out of his chair to kneel before her, with the quick grace that was so much a part of his attraction. He took her hands in his, and leaned towards her, his face darkly urgent.

'Lucy——' he said huskily, but at the sound of his voice the spell was broken. Lucy tore her hands from his and shrank back, turning her head away, and with a muttered oath Joss shot to his feet and returned to his chair. Lucy clasped her hands together to stop them shaking, cursing herself for being so foolhardy as to come back here, when the place had been the scene of so much pain in the past. Happiness too, she reminded herself, trying to be fair. The silence in the room lengthened, but it was different from before, no longer charged with sexual tension, and at last Lucy ventured a glance as Joss. He was staring into the fire with hooded eyes. The handsome face was set in bitter lines, and to her surprise Lucy felt an unexpected rush of sympathy. Casting about wildly for some neutral topic of conversation, she said the first thing that came to her head.

'I don't suppose you enjoy winter much in Abbotsbridge these days, Joss.' Even to her own ears this sounded inane in the extreme, and she flushed as Joss turned sardonic eyes in her direction.

'No, Lucy. And the weather is particularly bad for the time of the year, don't you agree? Quite the worst March night I remember.' His mouth twisted in a humourless smile. 'What would we British do without the weather to fall back on at awkward moments?'

'Perhaps that's why people in warmer, reliable climates have more volatile temperaments,' Lucy offered. 'No vagaries of weather to discuss as a safety valve.' To her relief, Joss's face relaxed a little, but he continued to look at her thoughtfully.

'What is it?' she asked. 'Have I changed so much?'

'Yes, you have.' His eyes took on a wary look. 'But that isn't what's on my mind.' He hesitated. 'I've no wish to intrude on your private affairs, Lucy, but has your father's death left you strapped for cash?'

'Since cash has never figured largely in my life anyway, it doesn't make much difference.'

'Isn't your shop doing well?' he asked quickly.

'Not badly at all, but——' Lucy stopped, colouring. 'I really mustn't bore you with my problems, Joss. When did you get back?'

Yesterday. I had rather hoped to see Tom

before he went.'

'You can see him when he's home next, if you're planning to be around for a while.' Lucy shifted uncomfortably in her chair.

Joss got up and stretched, looking large and rather overpowering in a bulky sweater and heavy cords. He shivered and bent to put more logs on the fire. 'You were right about the weather. I do feel the cold these days after my wanderings in hotter climates. It was enough to congeal the blood in your house tonight, Lucy. A fine old mess, one way and another.'

More mess than he knew, thought Lucy drearily, as she stared into the flames. What she needed was a magic lamp, complete with genie, to solve her problems. She started as she realised Joss was speaking to her.

'A drink, Lucy,' he repeated. 'You look as though you could do with one.'

He was right, she found. She badly needed something to give her courage, even if it were only of the Dutch variety. 'Scotch and soda, please,' she said absently, and Joss's teeth showed white in his dark face.

'A surprisingly masculine taste, Lucy.'

She shrugged. 'It's the only thing Dad ever kept in the house, so I used to have one now and then with him, to keep him company, *and* make sure he didn't indulge too much. His blood-pressure was a problem for the last year or so.' She accepted her drink with thanks and downed half of it in one swallow, to Joss's obvious amusement, glad of the spirit's warmth as it percolated through her. Suddenly she was struck by the improbability of the situation. She was in a house she'd sworn never to enter again, in company with a man she'd vowed never to speak to again in her entire life, and yet here they were, like a couple of old fogies, together by the fire as though it were something they did every night. Lucy smiled, and Joss eyed her quizzically.

'A real smile, Lucy? I was beginning to think you'd forgotton how.'

'It suddenly struck me how—how odd this is.'

'Breaking bread with the enemy?' Joss's eyes narrowed to a blue gleam. 'Perhaps you remembered too late you'd forgotten your long-handled spoon.'

'To sup with the devil!' Lucy laughed. 'Perhaps it isn't necessary just for sandwiches.'

'Bring it along tomorrow night and dine with me properly,' he said, taking her by surprise.

The laughter faded from her eyes. 'I don't think that's wise.'

'Where does wisdom come into it? I've been granted a God-sent chance tonight, by kind courtesy of the weather, to extend yet again my ever-ready olive branch.'

She looked at him steadily, trying to read his expression, but without success. 'I wish I could believe that this olive branch was tendered in good faith, Joss—or even that it was tendered to me. If you're honest, you'll admit it's Tom you're aiming at, not me.'

Joss shook his head, then finished his drink. 'Not,' he said carefully, 'that I *wouldn't* like to see more of Tom, naturally.'

'Why?'

'Because I'm very fond of him. Who wouldn't be?' Joss's face hardened. 'But you've always been very careful to keep us apart, Lucy, haven't you? To deny me any relationship with him beyond the odd hour or two once in a blue moon.'

Lucy's eyes were cold. 'But *you* were the one who denied the relationship, Joss. When you learned I was pregnant you made it crystal-clear I was never to name Simon as the father of my son. And I never have. Ever. You didn't want to be Tom's uncle eleven years ago, Joss. Do you honestly expect me to feel any sympathy for the fact that somewhere along the way you changed your mind? You said some pretty foul things to me. Unforgettable things.'

The colour receded from Joss's face, the look in his eyes touching some deep buried chord inside Lucy, despite herself.

'I was off my head with grief and shock,' he said. 'Caroline had run off with her Argentinian lover only days before Simon was killed, remember. My pride was still smarting from her defection on that God-awful afternoon when you rang from the aerodrome.'

'It was three weeks, in actual fact,' said Lucy.

He frowned at her. 'Three weeks? What are you talking about?'

'Caroline left you exactly three weeks before Simon was killed.'

'You remember it so clearly, then?'

'Oh, yes. You weren't exactly quiet and dignified about it. You were a drunken monster, in fact. One tends to remember things like that very clearly.'

'Does one, indeed?' Joss jumped up and made for the whisky decanter. 'Have another drink?'

Lucy opened her mouth to refuse, then shut it again and held out her glass.

'Couldn't we come to some amicable arrangement, Lucy?' Joss turned back to the drinks tray. 'Since your father died, Tom must surely be lacking in male companionship at home, if not in school. Is an hour or two with me now and then too much to ask?'

'Why don't you get married and have a son of your own?' she demanded. To her surprise, Joss's face darkened.

'I have my reasons,' he said stiffly, 'none of which I imagine would interest you in the slightest.'

Lucy stared at him, affronted, but he met her eyes levelly.

'Well?' he prompted. 'Are you going to let me see more of Tom in future, or not?'

She looked down at her hands as though she'd never seen them before, examining each fingernail with minute care for a long time. 'If Tom wants to,' she said at last, 'I won't prevent him from coming to visit you. But it's up to Tom.'

Joss rose to his feet and pulled her up from her chair, looking down at her intently. 'You mean it, Lucy?'

She nodded, and very gently he bent to touch his lips to her forehead.

'Thank you,' he said. 'It means a great deal to me. Almost as though Simon were back with me again.'

'You felt very differently once.' Which sounded petty, Lucy knew, but the hurt had cut too deep all those years ago to be forgotten so easily. 'If my father hadn't taken Tom fishing one day near your place you might never have come to know him at all.'

'One look, at him was enough, Lucy.' Joss

turned to lean a hand on the chimney piece, and stared down into the fire. 'Can you believe that I just *like* Tom? Even if he weren't Simon's son, I'd still feel exactly the same.'

'He doesn't *look* much like Simon,' Lucy pointed out. 'He's like Dad—and me.'

'Except for his eyes.' Joss turned to face her. 'Is it totally beyond your power to forgive me, Lucy?'

She regarded him thoughtfully. 'You ask a lot. I've conceded as far as Tom's concerned. Why should *my* forgiveness be so important?'

'Until tonight, I can't honestly say I thought it was.' Joss frowned, a look almost like surprise in his eyes. 'It all happened a long time ago, Lucy. Yet when I saw your car in the ditch tonight I felt as though someone had punched me in the stomach.'

'You mean, you thought Tom was with me?'

'No. That never even occurred to me. My only reaction was fear that you were hurt, and I drove like a bat out of hell to Holly Lodge—only to get mugged for my pains.'

'I thought you were an intruder. Besides, a chunk of ceiling had just fallen on me; you can't expect someone to behave perfectly rationally under those circumstances.' Lucy's gaze was serene. 'So. You had a fit of remorse and came round to play the good Samaritan, Joss. Well done, and thanks. And now I think I'll retire to that very charming room Mrs Benson gave me. It's Monday tomorrow—not my favourite day of the week at any time. Tomorrow it's likely to be worse than usual, worrying about things at the lodge.'

'Leave the keys with me and I'll chase up the plumber and the electrician.'

Lucy eyed him doubtfully. 'I don't want to put you to any trouble.'

Joss's smile lacked mirth. 'The least I can do, under the circumstances. God knows, you could do with some help.'

'Isn't that the truth!' Lucy smiled wryly and fished in her handbag for the keys. 'There. Now I'll say goodnight—and thank you again.'

Joss insisted on escorting her up to her room, and Lucy felt oddly awkward as he switched on the lights in the guest room and asked her if she had everything she needed.

'Everything,' she assured him hastily. 'Mrs Benson turned on the electric blanket earlier on, so what more can I ask?'

'Sleep well then, Lucy.' Joss hesitated, then bent and kissed her mouth. Lucy shot back as though he'd hit her.

'*Droit du seigneur*?' she asked, eyes glittering.

Joss's face darkened. 'Just a token of comfort, Lucy. Besides, to be pedantic, you're not precisely eligible for the *droit du seigneur* bit, are you? If you remember, when the lord of the manor exercised his right to take first turn in his underling's nuptial couch, the bride was expected to be a maiden.'

CHAPTER TWO

To SAY that Lucy spent a restless night was an understatement. Any thaw she had begun to feel towards Jonas Woodbridge froze up again at his parting shot, and she undressed in a temper which put paid to immediate thoughts of sleep. Besides, the room was too warm, there were too many clothes on the bed and Lucy, used to the more bracing temperatures of Holly Lodge, lay awake for a long time, fuming at first over Joss, then gradually calming down, her thoughts turning to Simon, and her father, and, inevitably, to Tom.

Her ten-year-old son was a normal, untidy boy with his father's eyes, his mother's dark, curly hair, and a passion for computers and cricket at the school his war-hero grandfather had once enlivened with his presence. And now Lucy and Tom were really on their own at last, since Thomas 'Bulldog' Drummond's sudden death shortly after Christmas. But it was only now, she thought despairingly, that she was really beginning to learn the meaning of life as a single parent. Until recently, she had always had her father behind her. Supportive but bracing, he had never allowed her to feel sorry for herself. It was left to the population of Abbotsbridge to feel sorry for Lucy Drummond, not just because she was pregnant at the tender age of seventeen, but because Simon Woodbridge, the only boyfriend Lucy had ever had, died before he could marry her.

There had been one bright spot in the whole tragic business. From the time she was fourteen years old Lucy had worked at weekends for Miss Cassandra Page at Abbotsbridge's one antiques shop, and it was to the eccentric, ageing woman that motherless Lucy first confided her secret. Imperturbable and reassuring, Cassie promptly offered a full-time job at the shop, baby in tow as well, when it arrived, and even volunteered to break the news to 'Bull' Drummond. But that gentleman hadn't been a war hero for nothing. After flying Lancaster bombers in countless sorties over Berlin, it never occurred to him to do other than comfort his distraught child and face the world with the news at once.

The one notable exception to the general sympathy and support was Jonas Woodbridge. Wild with grief over Simon and unaccountably furious with Lucy, he had let her know in no uncertain terms that she had no claim on him through Simon. There was no proof of paternity, he said with cruelty, lashing out in a way that utterly shattered the teenage Lucy. It made no difference to her that Jonas Woodbridge regained his sanity within hours. The damage, as far as Lucy was concerned, was well and truly done. Time after time Joss went to Holly Lodge to try to make amends, but Lucy was immovable. She would have none of him, and stonily told her father to send him away. Joss, she considered, was more fortunate than herself in several ways. Since he was a trained anthropologist, as well as heir to a considerable estate, he had the means to assuage his grief in his work, and could travel as far from

Abbotsbridge as he liked. Lucy, perforce, had to stay put and play the hand life had dealt her.

Lying wakeful and restless in the guest-room at Abbot's Wood, Lucy scowled blackly, resentful that nature had been so generous to Jonas Woodbridge, endowing him with a natural talent for writing, in addition to a spectacular body and handsome face. And as if that weren't enough, now it seemed Joss wanted Tom as well.

How much *would* Tom miss having a man around that he could turn to? Thank God he had his school for male companionship most of the time. And at least she had no worry about school fees. Her father had made provision for them until Tom was eighteen. By that time, perhaps, she would have discovered a forgotten Turner landscape in someone's attic and made a fortune. She would certainly have to find *some* means of putting Tom through college. Only the stock at the antiques shop was hers. She merely rented the actual premises, and the rent was the next bill looming large on the horizon. A good thing Joss had no idea how bad things really were, nor how dull and exemplary a life she led. Lucy sighed glumly. Here she was, twenty-eight years old, and, except for Tom, hardly ever having anything to do with any man at all now her father was dead. Which, no doubt, explained why sitting cosily by the fire this evening with Joss Woodbridge had been so surprisingly pleasant, in spite of the past. A pity he'd had to spoil it all with his goodnight kiss.

The kiss itself, she conceded, had not been objectionable. It was the motive behind it that got her on the raw. Lucy flung over on her back and stared at the ceiling. If she were honest, the touch of Joss's mouth on hers had shaken her badly. What a fool she was! After years of believing herself utterly immune to Joss Woodbridge's fabled charisma, the unacceptable truth was quite different. Seventeen-year-old Lucy had worshipped the very ground Joss trod. The merest touch of his hand had been enough to turn her bones to jelly. She was appalled to find it still did. No matter how much her brain repudiated Joss Woodbridge, her traitorous body responded to him shamelessly. Hormones, thought Lucy repressively; common-or-garden hormones, nothing more.

There were dark marks under Lucy's eyes next morning, but she left her face bare of make-up and tied her hair back with a black ribbon after she'd dressed in the black ski-pants and heavy fisherman's jersey brought with her to wear at the shop. Joss, she decided, must take her as she was. He was reading the paper at the breakfast table when she joined him. He was a bit dark under the eyes too, she noted, but on Joss's face it looked irritatingly good. In fact, he looked too attractive for words in a heavy white sweater and old denims.

'Good morning, Lucy.' He held out a chair for her, scrutinising her face closely as she sat down. 'You look tired. Wasn't the bed comfortable?'

'Too comfortable. I'm used to more Spartan conditions.' She smiled at him politely, but refused the platter of bacon and eggs he offered. 'No thanks, just toast.'

'You should make a habit of starting the day with a good breakfast, Lucy,' he said. 'You work hard, so how can you expect your body to function without fuel?'

'I eat well enough.' She poured coffee for them

both. 'Tom likes a cooked breakfast, but I can never face much at this hour.'

'What time do you open the shop?'

'I'm on my own on Mondays. It's a quiet day usually, so I unlock at about nine-thirty. There are very few tourists at this time of the year—not many customers at all, really, so I make use of Monday to dust and clean all the stock. I'm a bit low at the moment, so it's not as much of a chore as it can be.' Lucy halted as she saw Joss studying her face intently.

'You look terrible,' he said bluntly. 'Didn't you sleep at all?'

'Not much.'

'Are you worried about the lodge?'

Lucy nodded bleakly. 'I'm not having much luck with the sale. Not many people want a draughty Victorian house with no central heating —or if they do, they expect to get it for peanuts. And now, with all the mess from the bursts, it's worse than hopeless.'

Joss buttered some toast, frowning. 'Where do you intend to live when you do sell it?'

'Over the shop. It just isn't practical not to. It's included in my rent, anyway, and at the moment I just use the space for storage.' Lucy refused to meet his eyes.

'And Tom? What does he think about it?'

'Not much. But I've explained the situation and he realises we don't have any alternative.' Lucy smiled brightly. 'At least I'll be able to keep track of him during the school holidays.

'Cooped up in a couple of rooms over a shop! Not much fun for a lad of that age.'

It was not an over-enticing prospect for the lad's

mother, either, but Lucy refrained from saying so. None of it was any of Joss Woodbridge's business, even if he had taken it on himself to give her a bed for the night.

'You think I'm interfering,' observed Joss.

Lucy's face shuttered. 'Since you mention it, yes. I do.'

'Surely I have *some* right to show interest in your problems, Lucy?' His eyes locked with hers in a way which left her in no doubt as to his meaning, and she stared back frostily.

'I don't agree.' Lucy poured herself more coffee to give herself occupation, pleased to find her hand steady as she lifted the heavy silver pot.

'You felt differently once, Lucy,' said Joss quietly.

'I was very young. And very silly. I'm a lot older now, and hopefully a little bit wiser than—than I was when . . .' She trailed into silence, transfixed by the searching blue gaze trained on her.

'When we succumbed to a very violent mutual attraction despite that extreme youth of yours, Lucy?' His voice deepened and roughened, and Lucy tensed, her heart beating faster.

'This is no conversation for breakfast time,' she said curtly, wrenching her eyes from his with an effort. 'And if you had any shred of decency you'd leave that particular episode in the past where it belongs.'

From beneath lowered lids Lucy saw Joss lean back in his chair, apparently perfectly relaxed.

'Which particular episode?' he asked tauntingly. 'Do you mean all those times when I couldn't resist putting an arm around you, or pulling you on my knee just so I could hold you? Or do you mean the day when we were finally engulfed in a mutual

flood of infatuation—and ultimate guilt? Because
we *were* guilty, were we not, of various forms of
infidelity between us? You were Simon's property,
I was engaged to Caroline. And even if I hadn't
been, it really wasn't cricket to steal my brother's
sweetheart, was it?'

'You didn't *steal* me——'

'No. But I damn well seduced you, didn't I?'
Joss paused, and Lucy glared at him, jumping to
her feet, but he stayed her with a peremptory hand.
'No. Sit down again for a moment, please, Lucy.
While we're on this particular emotive subject I'd
like to know the truth about one thing. Do you
deny that, young though you were, you wanted me
in the same way?'

Lucy stared at him in silence. By no means in the
same way, she thougth. You lusted after *me*, but I
was fathoms deep in love with *you*. My idol. Too
bad you fell off your pedestal with such a crash.

'No, I don't deny it,' she said out loud. 'I had a
real schoolgirl crush on you, Joss. Subsequent
events cured it rather effectively, I'm afraid.'

His mouth curved in a mirthless smile. 'A fact
you made crystal-clear at the time. I grew tired of
beating a path to your door eventually, since it
remained so firmly shut in my face.'

Lucy eyed him curiously. 'Surely you didn't
expect anything else?'

The smile grew self-derisive. 'Shall we say I
hoped? There was something I wanted very badly
to say to you, but you wouldn't even let your father
ask me in the house.' He shrugged. 'I received, as
they say, my just deserts, one way and another. No
matter; it was all a long time ago.'

'Very true. So let's forget it, shall we?' Lucy

stood up. 'I'd better be off. If it's convenient for you to take me now,' she added stiffly.

Joss half rose automatically, then sat down again. 'Certainly. But I'd rather like to finish my coffee first.'

Lucy's chin rose. 'Of course. I'll just go upstairs and make sure I've left nothing behind.' She knew perfectly well she had not, but for the moment she badly needed an excuse to remove herself from Joss's vicinity. When she returned, he was waiting for her.

'Ready?' he asked, and waved a hand towards the window. 'Snowing again, I'm afraid.'

Lucy forgot the constraint between them and rushed to look out. 'Oh, lord! Perhaps I should go by the lodge; see what else has happened.'

'Unnecessary. I've had a word with Ted and he's sending someone along to deal with the plumbing and electricity, plus a mechanic from the garage to tow the car away. I'd advise you to get a claim form from your insurance people, Lucy.'

The words hit Lucy like a bodyblow. She murmured something unintelligible as they drove off down the long, fence-lined drive to the road, and said nothing else at all on the journey to Abbotsbridge. She let Joss lift her down from the Land Rover when they arrived, oblivious of the interested glances directed at them by several passers-by, and unlocked the door of the attractive, double-fronted antiques shop, which boasted bottle glass in its bow windows and a wrought-iron sign that creaked in the cold east wind.

'I'd better come in and check on your pipes here, too,' said Joss, and Lucy went white.

'Oh, my God, I never even gave it a thought——'
She flew through the shop and into the private
quarters at the back, taking the stairs two at a time
to the rooms above. When she found everything as
usual she felt limp with relief.

'Everything all right?' called Joss from the foot
of the stairs, and Lucy ran down again quickly.

'Yes, thank heavens.' She thrust a hand through
her hair. 'If there'd been water dripping all over
my precious stock I'd have had hysterics.'

Joss held out a bundle of letters. 'Your mail,
Lucy. I'll take myself off now I know all's well.'

'Joss——' Lucy hesitated, feeling awkward. 'I
do appreciate your help. Thank you for putting me
up last night.' Her eyes met his, her cheeks growing
warm as she saw the amusement in his eyes.

'You just hate being obliged to me for anything,
don't you, Lucy Drummond?' He touched her
cheek lightly. 'Don't work too hard. *Ciao*.'

'*Ciao*,' she echoed, and watched his tall figure
thread its way through desks and chests and tables
laden with objects of varying value. Lucy turned
away with a sigh to her tiny little office, and put the
kettle on for coffee to drink while she tackled the
mail. There were the usual leaflets and circulars,
plus the electricity bill for the shop and the bill for
the rent. Her eyes goggled as she saw the figure on
the statement. If Miss Drummond wished to renew
the agreement the new figure would be a fifty per
cent increase on the rent paid over the past few
years. Lucy sat down abruptly at her desk. She had
known an increase was in the offing, but not a sum
of such magnitude. She could manage it once she
had the money from the sale of Holly Lodge, but
since there were no takers at the moment, nor likely

to be until the ravages of yesterday had been repaired, she had no idea where the money was coming from. She already had a loan for stock from the bank, so there was no help from that quarter. Tom's fees were secure, admittedly, but boys grew out of clothes and needed all sorts of extras at school on top of them. And this was the dead season in the trade. No one was likely to come in this morning thirsting for a Victorian credenza, or a set of William the Fourth dining chairs.

What, Lucy wondered in desperation, was she to do? The only things of value were among her stock, but if she sold the stock at auction her livelihood was gone. Listlessly she gathered dusters and polish and set about her usual Monday cleaning, while her brain went round in circles, trying to devise some way out of her dilemma. Each window of the shop was furnished as nearly as possible as a room, with more attention paid to a pleasing effect to catch the customer's eye than strict adherence to value or period. Lucy dusted the George the Third bookshelves, smoothed the nap on a velvet chaise-longue, and retied the heavy silk cords holding back a swathe of damask curtain. She lingered lovingly over the inlay on a round French rosewood table, pulling out its satin-lined compartments for maximum effect, then gave a tweak to the horsehair mane of a rocking-horse with a saucy look in its eye.

'I'm glad *you* look cheerful, Pegasus,' she told him, and went on to dust the innumerable pieces of porcelain and glass dotted about, finishing her routine by polishing the glass cabinet displaying her collection of Victorian card-cases. The only customers during the morning were an elderly lady

wanting a pretty china soap dish, and a smart
young woman after a china jardinière for her
conservatory. But even two sales were more than
expected, Lucy consoled herself, as she eyed the
grey day outside. The snow had stopped, but it was
still very cold, and few people were about. Lucy
closed the shop at lunch time, went along to the
bakery for a cheese roll, and ate it at her desk while
she went through her books and juggled with
figures until her head ached, but no magic solution
presented itself. There was no escaping the fact
that she needed a loan from somewhere, and
needed it fast.

Lucy was still deep in calculations when the
telephone interrupted her.

'Lucy?' Joss's voice in her ear was unexpected.
'Are you busy?'

If only she were! 'No, Joss. What is it?'

'The electricity's back on at the lodge, but the
plumbing's unlikely to be sorted out today, I'm
afraid.'

Lucy felt guilty. She'd actually forgotten about
the mess at the lodge in her preoccupation with
figures. 'You really shouldn't have troubled, Joss;
I do apologise.'

'Don't be silly.' He sounded brusque. 'Your
car's been collected, and Stan Porter at the garage
will ring you tomorrow with the verdict. He wasn't
very optimistic, I should warn you.'

Lucy wasn't surprised. 'No, Joss, I don't
suppose he was, but thanks for letting me know.'

'What time do you close?'

'Fiveish.'

'Right. I'll pick you up then.'

Lucy frowned at the receiver. 'Really, you

needn't bother. I can walk.'

'Don't talk rot. I'll see you at five.' And Joss put an end to her protests by hanging up.

Lucy was nettled by his high-handed manner, but glad just the same that a long walk home in the dark didn't face her at the end of the day. Suddenly she sat bolt upright, struck by an electrifying idea, then shook her head violently. No. Out of the question. Jonas Woodbridge was no doubt in a position to lend her money—no one better in Abbotsbridge—but to ask him for a loan was going against every principle she possessed. But would principles buy Tom the new shoes he needed, or pay the repair bills at the lodge and cough up the money for the rent on the shop?

It would only be a temporary loan, said a wheedling voice in her brain. Just until she sold the lodge. She would make it clear she expected to pay the usual interest, of course. Joss Woodbridge wouldn't miss a few hundred pounds—Lucy frowned. More like a couple of thousand, really, if she paid all the bills as well.

No! Lucy jumped to her feet, shoving away her ledgers. She could never bring herself to ask. The words would stick in her throat. At one time she had sworn never to speak to him again, so what on earth was she doing even contemplating asking him for a loan?

Lucy made a few sales during the afternoon, to her surprise. Nothing very momentous; one of the card-cases, some of the special wax polish she made herself, a nice little watercolour. More than she could have expected on a cold, snowy Monday, but nothing like enough to allay her terrible anxiety. By the time Joss appeared promptly at five

Lucy was heartily glad to set the burglar alarm and lock up the shop.

'Good day?' Joss asked, as he helped her into the Land Rover.

'Like the curate's egg: good in parts.' Lucy sighed deeply as they moved off.

'You sound depressed,' Joss commented.

'Sorry.'

'And my news won't cheer you up, I'm afraid.' Lucy braced herself. 'What now?'

'Most of the pipes need renewing at Holly Lodge before you can expect the house to pass a surveyor's examination, which any purchaser would expect.' Joss glanced down at her. 'Your insurance should cover most of it, of course——'

'I let it lapse,' blurted Lucy.

'You did *what*?'

'I couldn't manage it, Joss. The insurance on the shop was more pressing. I was going to try to pay it next month, but—but——' She paused, trying to steady her voice. 'I just can't claim on the insurance. I'll have to find the money for the plumbing myself.'

Joss swore softly as they left the lights of the town behind. 'Lucy, the house isn't habitable. Some of the pipes have sheered clear away, and the plumber advises re-routing the entire system to the first floor instead of leaving them up in the loft where they could ice up again.'

'Oh, my God!' Lucy sat stunned. 'But won't that mean new floorboards and masses of redecorating, and——' She trailed into silence as they drew up at the gates of Holly Lodge, staring malevolently at the For Sale sign, which seemed to taunt her as Joss lifted her down.

Inside the house there was now light. And Lucy could have wished there was not. Candlelight had veiled the full horror of the damage the evening before. Now it was revealed in all its depressing detail: the stained ceiling and walls in the hall, the ruined carpet, and the whole atmosphere was prevalent with damp. Upstairs the debris of the fallen ceiling had been cleared away, and Lucy took one look at the gaping places overhead and sat down abruptly on the top stair.

'Not a pretty sight, it is?' She tried to smile at Joss.

'Not to put too fine a point on it, Lucy, it's bloody awful. Get your things together.' He started back downstairs, and Lucy sprang to her feet to run after him.

'What do you mean?' she demanded.

'You're coming home with me,' he said flatly. 'Go and pack.'

'I can't do that! I'm not walking out of here and leaving everything in this state. This is my home!' She threw out her hands in appeal.

Joss's face took on the type of expression parents wear to deal with fractious offspring. 'You can't live here until the place is dry again, Lucy. Be sensible.'

Lucy knew he was right, but resentment at his tone made her obstinate. 'Very well, but I don't have to impose on *you*. I can stay with Perdy.' She brushed past him and went into the kitchen to dial Perdy's number, but after a couple of rings a male voice answered.

'Is—is Perdita there?' asked Lucy, taken aback.

'Sure. Who shall I say wants her?' asked the cheerful voice.

'Lucy Drummond.'

In seconds Perdy's voice was gurgling down the line, full of suppressed excitement in a way Lucy recognised with a sinking heart.

'Lucy, love? How's things?' Without waiting for an answer, Perdy rushed on like a stream in full spate. 'Just got back. Divine weekend in this fabulous little inn tucked away in the back of beyond in the Cotswolds and—guess what?— Paul's come back with me! He's—er—going to stay for a while. Don't worry,' she added hastily, 'I'll be in to help at the shop as usual. You'll spare me for an hour or two, darling, won't you?' she said in muffled voice to someone at the other end. There was a smothered giggle, then Perdy said breathlessly, 'Everything OK with you, Lucy? Tom get back all right?'

'Yes,' said Lucy brightly. 'Tom's fine.'

'Anything in particular you wanted?'

'No, no—just thought I'd check you were back for tomorrow afternoon.'

'Sure thing, darling. See you.'

Lucy put the telephone down and turned to face Joss. He leaned in the doorway, looking large and formidable.

'I didn't hear you beg a bed for the night, Lucy.'

'No. It was only going to be a temporary bunk on a sofa anyway, but Perdy has a friend staying with her.' Lucy smiled philosophically. 'It doesn't matter. Now the electricity's back, there's no reason why I can't stay here.'

'Other than catching pneumonia!' Joss shivered. 'God, the damp's getting to my bones just standing here. For pity's sake, pack a bag and come home with me, Lucy, before we both get a chill.'

'You can go. I'm staying.' Lucy's face took on a mulish look as she folded her arms in defiance.

'They haven't turned the water on, Lucy, so you can't cook much, or make tea, or have a bath. *And,*' he added, folding his arms in imitation, 'I don't propose to stir a step until you decide to come with me.'

'Why all the sudden concern?' she demanded angrily. 'For years you haven't even acknowledged my existence——'

'*Your* choice, not mine. I kept track of you all right, Lucy. Besides, until recently I always knew your father was there to look after you.'

'I don't need anyone to look after me!'

'No?' His eyes held her deliberately and Lucy flushed.

'This—this present state of affairs is only temporary. Normally I'm perfectly self-sufficient. If it hadn't been for the weather, none of this would have happened. One can't foresee acts of God!'

Joss moved towards her. 'True. But one *can* accept help when it's offered. Even when it comes from a man you persist in casting as villain of the piece.'

'With reason.' Lucy eyed him challengingly.

Joss shrugged. 'I'm not denying I behaved badly towards you on that one occasion, but there were extenuating circumstances. And I very quickly tried to make amends. After ten long years, Lucy, can't you find it in your heart to be gracious enough to accept a little help from me? Particularly when it's obvious you need it so badly.'

Lucy's shoulders sagged. What on earth was she making such a fuss about? she thought wearily.

Pride was an expensive commodity. She just couldn't afford it. And it would be pretty stupid to push away Joss's olive branch with one hand, then stretch out the other in request for a loan. Because suddenly she knew that was what she was going to do. If Tom's security depended on her swallowing her pride to ask Jonas Woodbridge for a loan there was no question of doing anything else. For Tom's sake, she told herself. So do it.

'All right, Joss,' she said quietly. 'I'll come. Thank you. But just until the house is fit to live in, of course.'

Joss put out a hand and smoothed her hair, which was curling wildly in the cold, damp air. 'Poor Lucy. That took a lot of effort, didn't it?'

Lucy dodged away. 'You know it did,' she said with passion, 'so don't rub it in. I'll pack a few things. Shan't be long.'

Joss opened the door for her. 'Don't rush. We've all the time in the world.' He smiled down at her lazily.

Lucy frowned at him in suspicion, then ran up the stairs, her feet squelching on the sodden carpet. She'd forgotten that old trick of Joss's, of saying one thing and seeming to mean something else. It had infuriated Caroline. Poor Caroline. Or perhaps rich Caroline, if her polo-playing lover was wealthy. She'd been so beautiful, and so very condescending to 'Simon's little friend'. To a seventeen-year-old with frizzy, unmanageable hair, an assertive nose and too much bust, Caroline had been the absolute epitome of blonde, slender glamour. She had ignored Lucy, it was true, but at the same time fiercely resented Joss's predilection for his brother's little friend. Once she had Manuel

Vilas as an alternative resource, she took to taunting Joss about it behind Simon's back, taking care that Lucy should hear her offensive comments on men who hankered after little girls.

How suddenly everything had changed that summer, thought Lucy. Looking back, it seemed as though one moment everything had been sunshine and fun and the heady delight of illicit first love. Then Nemesis had overtaken Lucy Drummond and Joss Woodbridge, and nothing was ever the same. Caroline had a flaming row with Joss and left him for her handsome Argentinian, and Joss had taken to the bottle, while Lucy avoided him like the plague. Poor Simon had been utterly bewildered by the change in everyone. Lucy's eyes darkened. Poor Simon indeed; so tragically young to have all that laughter and life snuffed out on a glorious summer afternoon. Because it was his solo flight, Simon had persuaded her to go with him to watch, and she had been a horrified witness to it all. The tiny plane had soared up into the blue then plummeted to the ground, while Lucy stood rooted to the spot in shock as flames rose in a fiery ball above the hill where the plane crashed. And afterwards it had been Lucy who was given the thankless task of ringing Joss to tell him that his brother had been killed. And killed, what was more, during one of the forbidden flying lessons Simon had saved up for in secret.

'Lucy!' called Joss, jerking her back to the present. 'I'm freezing. Are you ready?'

As I'll ever be, she muttered to herself, and snapped her case shut and ran downstairs.

CHAPTER THREE

MRS BENSON took Lucy's return for granted, scolding at the mere idea of staying in a damp, cold house when there was room and to spare at Abbot's Wood.

'But it must mean extra work for you,' said Lucy, as she hung her clothes up in the pretty guest-room.

'Not a bit of it,' said the housekeeper. 'Mr Joss wouldn't even let me cook dinner tonight. He's taking you out for a meal.'

Oh, is he? thought Lucy.

'You didn't mention we were dining out,' she told Joss when she joined him in the study later. 'I haven't brought anything very grand in the way of clothes.' For the simple reason that she didn't possess any.

Joss looked at her plain red wool dress and smiled. 'You look perfect, Lucy. No frills. Just right.'

Lucy's purchases never ran to frills, because plain clothes had less tendency to date. Tonight, however, she had pinned her mother's garnet brooch to one shoulder, as a gesture to frivolity.

'I didn't mention eating out because I prefer to avoid arguments whenever possible. And you *are* rather inclined to argue, Lucy. Admit it.' Joss grinned at her and waved a hand at the tray of drinks on the desk. 'Anything here appeal to you?'

Lucy accepted a glass of dry sherry and raised it in toast. 'To my rescuer.'

Joss eyed her narrowly. 'Why, thanks Lucy. How unusually magnanimous of you.'

'A guest should be polite to her host.' Lucy smiled up at him, surprising an odd expression in his eyes. 'I'm sorry if I was—well, difficult at first.'

'Are you, Lucy?' He looked doubtful. 'I can't help feeling there's a reason for your capitulation.'

Lucy took a sip of sherry to cover her dismay. Was the man a mind-reader? 'I decided it was the best thing to do, that's all.'

'Good. Because for a week or so Holly Lodge is likely to be uninhabitable.'

Lucy stared at him in consternation. '*That* long?' She breathed out slowly. 'Then may I ring Tom's housemaster, please? I'd better let him know my whereabouts.'

'Of course.' Joss finished his drink. 'I'll just have a word with Benson while you make your call.'

Lucy got through to Tom's housemaster, explained her change of address briefly, and when Joss returned she was prowling round the bookshelves, looking at his catholic selection of literature.

'Shall we go then, Lucy?' Joss smiled at her, and Lucy's heart contracted. Simon's smile had been just like that. She blinked and smiled back.

'Ready when you are. Though I don't quite see why you have to entertain me. I'm not really a guest.'

'Just be quiet and enjoy the evening without arguing,' said Joss severely, and helped her on with her coat. He drew the collar together under her chin and looked down into her eyes. 'Unless, of course, you feel an evening with me is something to be endured rather than enjoyed?'

Taken off guard, Lucy shook her head, colouring.

'No. Of course not, Joss. Besides,' she added candidly, rather spoiling the effect, 'I don't get taken out for a meal all that often, so I'm bound to enjoy it, if only for the novelty.'

'Thanks a lot, Lucy!' Joss's smile was wry as they went out to the Land Rover. 'My ego's taking a terrible hammering, you know!'

'Sorry,' Lucy muttered when they were on their way. 'It's the truth, though.'

'Which has a nasty habit of being unpalatable!' He laughed, and Lucy smiled to herself in silent agreement.

Jonas Woodbridge was obviously well known in the restaurant, which Lucy mistook for a private house when they arrived. Outside there were thick stone walls and leaded windows. Inside there were two rooms conected by a wide arch, with real log fires burning in twin fireplaces with marble surrounds. Relieved of her humble sheepskin, Lucy felt less out of place in her plain dress than expected. The other women diners were dressed for warmth, as she was, though she felt certain hers was the only chainstore dress in the room.

'Do you like it here?' asked Joss, when they were settled at one of the tables.

'How could I not? It's a beautiful place, Joss.' Lucy eyed the giltwood sphinxes flanking the nearest fireplace. 'Unless I'm much mistaken, those are genuine French First Empire,' she said impressed, and smiled mischievously at Joss. 'I only hope you don't have to contribute to their value when you pay the bill!'

He laughed, his teeth white in his dark face, and Lucy was amused to see several female heads swivel in their direction. 'If I do, it's worth it,' he assured her. 'The food here is inspired.'

Lucy relaxed, settling down to enjoy the evening. To let it blank out her problems for a few sybaritic hours. 'Yummy,' she said blissfully, as they pored over the menu presented to them. 'What do you recommend?'

Joss looked at her whimsically. 'Although I've known you since you were a chubby urchin with braces on your teeth, Lucy, I'm sad to say I have no idea of your taste—except in antique furniture. Are you a vegetarian, or a devotee of *cuisine minceur*, or do you just eat a little of everything in moderation?'

Lucy's eyes sparkled as she sipped her sherry. 'A run-down on my sort of cuisine, Jonas Woodbridge, would probably give you indigestion even to listen, due to its basic components of wholemeal bread and baked beans!' She scanned the menu again with unconcealed avidity. 'Just about anything on here would meet with my approval!' As she glanced up at him, smiling, she surprised an expression of something very like pain in the hard blue eyes watching her, and she flushed as Joss reached out to touch her hand very fleetingly with his.

'I'll take you at your word, then,' he said lightly, and beckoned the hovering waiter to take their order.

It was, thought Lucy as she ate, quite the most superb meal she had eaten in her entire life. The warmth from the fire, the attentive service, the discreet buzz of conversation from the other diners all contributed to her intense enjoyment of the broccoli mousse and sharp hollandaise sauce, the ragout of scallops and mussels contained in a light-as-air rectangle of puff pastry, the cleverly presented fresh vegetables.

'You approve?' asked Joss, who hadn't succeeded in getting a word out of her for some time.

Lucy laid down her knife and fork with a blissful sigh. 'Exquisite. I've never eaten food remotely like it.'

'Don't you eat out at all?' Joss leaned forward to refill her glass with Montagny Premier Cru.

Lucy shook her head. 'Not since Dad died. And then it was usually a pub lunch with Tom somewhere on *exeat* weekends and in the holidays.'

Joss frowned. 'But surely you've been out with males other than your father and Tom, Lucy?'

'Yes. Once in a blue moon.' She met his eyes head on. 'But I have to be very careful, you know. No living it up in any way, or—or one-night stands, or anything. As an unmarried lady with a ten-year-old son, I lead an exemplary life from sheer necessity. I earn my living in Abbotsbridge and I'm dependent on the good will of the town. My one slip was received with sympathy, but I fancy another wouldn't go down well at all.'

'Do you still feel hostile towards me, Lucy?' he asked quietly.

Lucy thought it over carefuly. 'No. Not really, Joss. Of course, I won't deny you didn't add to my general well-being at the time by being so bloody-minded about my pregnancy. I wasn't thrilled to bits about it myself. Seventeen and scared silly, and full of guilt and grief over Simon; one way and other I had enough on my plate without the scorching you gave me.'

Joss stared down into his empty glass. 'I had no

right to do it, I know. My only excuse is that I was of "unsound mind" at the time.'

'You certainly got the wrong end of the stick. I wanted——' she stopped dead and he looked up in surprise. 'I wanted sympathy, not money,' she went on, which was not the entire truth. She had wanted more than that—much more—but had no intention of telling him exactly how much. 'The idea of financial help from you never entered my head.' Once again she checked herself. If there was any hope of enlisting Joss's help in the shape of a loan, she might do well to exercise more tact. She smiled at him cheerfully. 'Don't let's go over all that again, Joss. Leave it where it belongs—in the past. Now—could I have a pudding, please?'

Joss's involuntary crack of laughter attracted more female glances, which Lucy considered only natural. Joss had always possessed an utterly infectious laugh. Nowadays, she had an idea it wasn't heard all that often.

The sombre mood passed in the pleasure of decisions over hot ginger soufflé or creamy bread-and-butter pudding. Lucy decided on the former while Joss ate Cashel Blue cheese from Ireland, and from there on they kept by common consent to talk of Joss's travels, of Lucy's forays into the local countryside on treasure hunts for pieces to sell in her shop, and her friend Perdy Roche, who gave Lucy a hand at Abbotsbridge Antiques.

'Perdy nearly always has some male in tow—she attracts them like flies.'

'And is that what you'd really like to do?' asked Joss over coffee. 'Attract men like flies?'

Lucy grinned. 'With my sort of face? Not to mention a ten-year-old son! Although,' she added

reminiscently, 'Tom's housemaster was quite
attentive at first, because he assumed I was a
widow. When he learned I was a single lady he
cooled off rapidly. Unsuitable for a housemaster's
wife, I suppose.'

Joss eyed her closely. 'And would you have liked
to be?'

'Good heavens, no!' Lucy pulled a face. 'Not
my scene at all. I may grumble about my life-style,
but I enjoy most of it. I get to meet quite a lot of
people in the course of my travels. A lunch-time
drink and a sandwich with a group of other dealers
happens now and then, but apart from the
propriety bit I hardly ever go out at night, even if
asked. I get too tired by that time.'

'It's wrong!' said Joss forcefully.

Lucy's eyes opened wide. 'What is?'

'You shouldn't *be* too tired to enjoy yourself at
your age, Lucy.' Joss leaned towards her urgently.
'You're only a girl, for God's sake.'

She shook her head. 'I don't feel like a girl, Joss.
I think of myself as Tom's mother. And I feel
guilty because I miss him so much. It's very selfish
of me, because he loves his school, and anyway,
my father was adamant that Tom went away for
his education. I think Dad was afraid I'd get too
dependent on my son, or something. Turn him into
a mother's boy.'

Joss smiled involuntarily. 'From what I know of
Tom, that seems unlikely. But don't you think
your father wanted Tom to have the benefit of a
school where his grandfather's name counted for
something?'

Lucy looked at him, surprised. 'Dad told you
that?'

'No. It was just something I assumed all along. If a boy doesn't have a father, it must help his standing in a school if he had a grandfather there before him who was a legendary bomber pilot and an escaped prisoner-of-war, and so on. I imagine Bull Drummond was trying to give Tom the best start he could.'

'How perceptive of you, Joss. My father's sentiments exactly. Though how he ever managed to find the money for Tom's covenant I'll never know.' Lucy's smile was wry. 'Dad was inclined to live for the day otherwise, letting tomorrow take care of itself.' She looked at her watch. 'Lord—it's late. Would you mind if we went—went back, now?'

Joss rose promptly, a mocking little smile playing at the corners of his mouth. 'Careful,' he murmured in her ear as they left their table. 'You almost said "home" then.'

Lucy's cheeks were warm as Joss paid the bill and led her outside into the freezing darkness. Light flakes of snow were falling, and Joss tucked a rug round Lucy's knees for the journey, which needed his full concentration as he drove back to Abbot's Wood.

'I'm glad you're at the wheel,' said Lucy with feeling. 'My drive home last night has put me off motoring for a while.'

'Are you nervous now?' he asked.

'No.' Which was the truth, thought Lucy, surprised. In spite of the weather, she felt perfectly safe with Joss.

'You need a decent car,' he said. 'That old banger of yours has just about had it.'

He was only confirming what Lucy knew very

well already, but his words were depressing. At the
same time, they strengthened her resolve regarding
a loan. There was nothing for it; she would just
have to swallow her pride and ask Joss for the
money as prettily as possible. And as soon as
possible. Like the moment they got back.
Otherwise, Lucy knew only too well, she would
spend another sleepless night in Joss Woodbridge's
comfortable, too-warm guest-room.

When they got back, the Bensons were in bed,
but a tray stood ready in the study, with an
insulated jug of coffee and some home-made
biscuits.

'Or would you prefer a drink, Lucy?' asked
Joss.

'No, thanks. It would spoil the memory of that
wine we had with the meal.' Lucy smiled
diffidently. 'Thank you, Joss. It was a quite
wonderful dinner.'

'Good,' he said briskly, and handed her a cup of
coffee. 'I'm glad you enjoyed it. Biscuit?'

Lucy refused regretfully, too replete even for one
of Mrs Benson's famous biscuits that Simon had
loved so much.

'How about some music?'

'No, thank you.' Lucy took a deep breath. She
had to ask now or her courage would fail her, she
knew. 'Joss, there *is* something I want.'

He looked at her tense face and sat down. 'Yes,
Lucy? What is it?'

She licked suddenly dry lips and looked down at
her hands, which were trembling, she noted
absently. The coffee was slopping over into the
saucer, and she replaced the cup carefully on the
small table beside her. 'I need to ask you a favour,

Joss,' she said in a rush of desperation. 'A big
favour. I wouldn't, believe me, if I could think of
any other way.'

Joss's eyes were watchful, but his quiet 'Go on,'
was encouraging.

She cleared her throat. 'I need to borrow some
money, Joss.' There. It was out.

'I see.' His face was as informative as a sheet of
blank paper. 'I assume that I'm the last resort, that
you must have considered more conventional ways
of borrowing what you need.'

Lucy nodded miserably, then made a clean
breast of her troubles, of how her father had left
nothing except the house and its contents, and the
money for Tom's school fees. She gave him details
of the bank loan she was trying to reduce, her bills
for overheads, the increase in the shop's rent, and
finally the disaster of the car and the repairs to the
house.

'All I have of value,' she ended wearily, 'is the
stock at the shop. And if I sell that I have no way
of earning a living. Frankly, I don't know where to
turn, Joss.'

'So you turned to me.' His voice was
uninflected, but Lucy squirmed inwardly as she
met his eyes.

'If you hadn't arrived out of the blue at Holly
Lodge I'd never have thought of doing so,
obviously.' She bit her lip, conscious she was
putting things badly. 'I haven't seen you in ages—I
mean, you're so often out of the country . . .' She
trailed into silence and drank her cooling coffee.

'What sort of sum did you have in mind, Lucy?'

She looked up. 'Would—could you see your way
to lending about two thousand pounds, Joss?

Everything businesslike of course, with the usual interest——'

'Lucy, you're not being realistic,' he interrupted. 'Have you really thought this through?'

'I know it's a lot of money——'

'But it isn't. That's the point. It isn't anything like enough.' The finality in Joss's voice struck despair into Lucy's heart.

'You mean I need to borrow more?'

He nodded. 'The house will take that much at the very least to put it back in shape. And you're going to need a new car. I had a word with Stan Porter while you were dressing. He says yours isn't worth patching up.'

This was so much worse than Lucy had imagined she felt sick. 'But, Joss, I can't afford a new car. It isn't as though I can manage with a small one. I need an estate car for buying things to sell in the shop.'

'In your present state of finance can you even afford any more stock for the shop?' The blue eyes held hers, and Lucy shook her head slowly, feeling as though her world were falling to bits about her. She tried to assimilate what he'd said, but the truth was so unpalatable her numb brain refused to accept it.

'I believe I can provide a solution,' Joss said quietly.

Lucy's breath caught. 'What is it?'

His smile was sardonic. 'I hope you won't be too displeased, Lucy, but I think it's time to confess I intended asking a favour of you tonight, too.'

She straightened in her chair, eyeing him warily. 'Is that why you bought me such an expensive dinner? As a softening-up process?'

'You could have refused to come! But yes, that was partly my motive. Strange, isn't it? We each possess something the other wants. Surely it must be possible to come to some arrangement?'

Lucy stared at him in growing suspicion. '*My* requirements are embarrassingly obvious. I need money, and presumably you have enough of it to lend me what I need.'

'Give, Lucy, not lend.' He smiled as her dark eyes opened wide.

'*Give*?' she echoed. 'Did you say *give*?'

He nodded calmly. 'I'm prepared to take over the loan from the bank, pay your rent for the shop, the repairs to Holly Lodge and the cost of a new car.'

'And what can I possibly give you in return?' asked Lucy with foreboding. 'You can't be in need of a few sticks of antique furniture, and I'm sure my body isn't what you're after, either.'

Joss reached down and pulled her to her feet, holding her by the wrists. She trembled suddenly at the look in his eyes.

'I want Tom,' he said simply.

CHAPTER FOUR

COLOUR surged in Jonas Woodbridge's handsome face, while Lucy turned deathly pale.

'Are you suggesting I *sell* you my son?' she asked in brutal directness.

Joss's mouth curved in distaste, his fingers tightening on her wrists. 'This isn't a Thomas Hardy novel, Lucy. Do me the courtesy of listening carefully to what I have in mind as an acceptable transaction between us.'

'So this *is* a business deal, whichever way you wrap it up.' She pulled her hands free and rubbed absently at the red imprints his fingers had made on her wrists.

'I'm sorry, Lucy,' he said distantly. 'I didn't mean to mark your skin.'

She brushed this aside. 'I think I *will* have that drink, Joss, after all. Scotch and soda, please.'

While Joss turned away to pour the drinks, Lucy sat down rather suddenly. Her legs were demonstrating an annoying lack of support. She thanked him for the drink and took a sip of it to steady herself.

'Right,' she began briskly, as Joss sat down. 'Explain what you have in mind. Not,' she added, 'that it means I'll have anything to do with it. But, since you spent so much money on the dinner to put me in an amenable mood, it seems only fair I

58

should at least give you a hearing.' Her desperation about the enormity of her need had diminished somewhat in the face of Joss's proposition. She eyed him curiously, wondering if he could possibly be as unemotional as he looked. His face wore such a dispassionate expression, they might have been about to discuss some abstruse, legal matter concerning two other people.

'In simple terms, Lucy, I want an heir,' he said quietly. 'I'm not in the least fired with ambition to found a dynasty, but I would like someone with Woodbridge blood in their veins to have this place when I go. Who better than Tom? I like Tom. And I'm very grateful that you've allowed me to see something of him over the last three or four years.'

'He likes *you*. Otherwise I wouldn't have. Besides,' added Lucy honestly, 'it was my father who persuaded me to let you see something of him.'

'I see.' Joss's flexible mouth went down at the corners. 'I should have realised that. I was actually foolish enough to hope you might be thawing towards me.'

Lucy had no answer to that, and Joss was quiet for a while before continuing.

'You know how badly I took Simon's death, Lucy. Over and above the grief, I felt such guilt, I couldn't live with myself.'

'Guilt?' she queried, startled.

'I was Simon's guardian, remember, not just his brother. He was only a small boy when my father left him in my care. But that summer I was so taken up with fighting what I felt for you, and the subsequent fights with Caroline over it, that I was too blind to see what was happening under my nose.' Joss's magnificent eyes lit with such a cold, burning look, a tremor ran down Lucy's spine. 'If I hadn't flatly refused to let Simon have the flying lessons, perhaps things would have been different.' His smile was scathing. 'All those afternoons he made out he was spending with you, of course, he was working in the offices at the aerodrome to pay for the damn lessons. And you covered for him, Lucy. Pulled the wool over my eyes completely. It never entered my head you would lie to me.'

'I didn't, Joss.' Lucy's eyes dropped. 'Simon said he would tell the lies. My sin was in letting him.'

He breathed in sharply. 'And that wasn't all you let Simon do, was it, Lucy? Somewhere during those weeks he must have spared time from those flying lessons of his to give you lessons of a rather different kind. Were they better than mine, Lucy?'

Lucy glared at him. 'That is something I'm not prepared to discuss. If you carry on, I shall walk out of your house right now and make sure you never see Tom again.' Something in her manner plainly convinced Joss she meant what she said, and she took great pleasure in watching the effort he made to regain his composure before he could go on.

'To be brief, Lucy, all that's left of Simon are a few trophies from school, a few photographs, and Tom.'

There was a tense silence. 'I gather,' Lucy said at last, 'that you want me to acknowledge you legally as Tom's uncle.'

Joss shook his head. 'No, Lucy. But I'm willing to settle all your debts if you allow me to become Tom's stepfather.'

Lucy gaped at him, thunderstruck, and Joss smiled at her with infuriating indulgence as he leaned back in his chair, relaxed. 'That's right, Lucy. In other words, I'm asking you to marry me.'

She shook her head in wonder. 'You must want Tom very badly.'

'Don't sell yourself short! I'm quite happy to take you as part of the deal.'

Lucy's brain flatly refused to cope with this. 'I think you'd better spell it out in words of one syllable, Joss. I can't adjust to the fact that you want me as a wife. If you cast your mind back, you may recall that you were pretty insulting on the subject of my child's paternity when I told you I was pregnant.'

'Is that so hard to understand? It was just a simple case of jealousy, Lucy. I was so bloody jealous, I lashed out at you in the way I knew would hurt most.' Joss's face darkened with self-disgust. 'Besides, I badly needed someone to blame, didn't I? I had to find a scapegoat. Anyone but me. And you were the one who not only helped Simon sneak off behind my back to learn to fly, but actually let him make you pregnant, even after you and I—oh, what the hell! I'm not proud of myself, Lucy. After you ran away from me that day, I would have given my soul to retract the things I'd said to you, once I was functioning normally again.'

Joss sprang up and made for the decanter, then changed his mind, and put his empty glass down on the tray. 'So,' he said, turning to face her. 'What have you to say to my offer, Lucy? *Will* you come and live here as my wife, and let me share in bringing up Tom?'

Lucy looked at him thoughtfully. 'Would that include sharing your bed, Joss?'

His eyes mocked her. 'Is the prospect so very daunting?'

'Since I haven't given it any thought, I don't really know. But I told you I'd need everything spelled out for me. I would prefer to know what I was agreeing to. *If* I agreed to it, that is,' she added. 'Because, if Tom doesn't like the idea, I'm afraid no amount of debt would influence me to say yes. It's Tom you really want, so if he doesn't fancy you as a stepfather I'm afraid the whole thing's pretty pointless, isn't it?'

A pulse throbbed at the corner of Joss's mouth. 'And if Tom approves of the idea? Will you consent?'

Lucy thought it over, while several seconds ticked by on the French enamel clock on the shelf over the fire. Joss watched her frowning face, his own set in tense lines, until at last it was plain he could stand the suspense no longer.

'Well?' he demanded.

Lucy sighed, resigned. 'Very well, Joss. I suppose I must say yes. I don't see any other course open to me.'

Mockery replaced the tension on Joss's face. 'There you go again, Lucy, cutting my ego to ribbons. It does damn all for a man's self-esteem to be thought of as the last resort, I might tell you.'

'It must be the first time,' said Lucy, unmoved. 'With your looks, you must have had women falling at your feet all your life, Jonas Woodbridge.'

'Caroline, you may remember, ran off with

someone else!'

'And I know just why,' Lucy said without thinking, then stopped, biting her lip.

Joss sat down again, crossing his long legs as he smiled at her affably. 'Do you, now! I never knew Caroline confided in you, Lucy.'

'Oh, she didn't. She didn't like me at all. But after one of your more spectacular set-to's that summer she almost ran over me one day, when I was cycling here to see Simon. She jumped out of her car, dusted me off, then gave me some unsolicited advice.'

'What was it?' asked Joss, fascinated.

Lucy frowned, trying to remember the exact words. 'Looking back, I think she was warning me off. She told me not to be misled by your—er—predilection for me, and not to waste any time on a man who was—and I quote—so bloody erudite, he didn't understand that a woman wants more fun and—well—bed, than you had time for when you were engrossed in writing your deadly books about mouldy old natives.'

Joss threw back his head and laughed, running a hand through his thick brown hair. 'Poor Caroline! There was very little grey matter under that spectacular exterior. I hope Manuel the Magnificent, as Simon called him, has managed to supply all the fun and "bed" that she wanted.' He sobered suddenly. 'Caroline's opinion isn't much of a reference, is it? But without disclosing too many personal details, it was my preoccupation with you that drove her wild. Besides which she was a woman with too much time on her hands, and too little intellect to find something to do with it.'

'So how did you come to get engaged to her?'

asked Lucy, then coloured. 'I'm sorry. I've no right to ask personal questions.'

Joss shrugged. 'Who better? And I suppose I was attracted for the usual reasons at first: the icing on the cake. Unfortunately, I realised all too soon there wasn't enough common interest for actual marriage. Which, oddly enough, didn't make it any better for my vanity when she ran off with Manuel Vilas.'

'Your vanity must have been soothed by a fair bit of feminine reassurance since!'

'Some. But I've never even contemplated risking matrimony. Until now.' His eyes locked with hers, and Lucy fidgeted.

'You must have a great fondness for Tom to take the risk this time,' she muttered.

'I have. But is it so difficult to believe I'm fond of *you*, Lucy, as well as Tom?' He smiled faintly. 'I always was, as you very well know. It isn't as though we're strangers.' Abruptly he rose to his feet, holding out his hands. 'You must be exhausted, Lucy. Come on—let's go to bed.'

To her intense mortification, Lucy flushed bright red, and Joss pulled her out of her chair, laughing.

'Separately, of course, Lucy!'

She stalked upstairs ahead of him, very much on her dignity, until Joss caught her wrist as they reached the door of her room.

'Lucy—how soon can you arrange to see Tom?' The urgency in his voice touched her, in spite of herself.

'He's not due home on *exeat* for another three weeks, Joss. But I suppose if I ask special permission I could drive down next Sunday and take him out to lunch . . .' She halted, realising she had no car.

'Borrow one of the cars here,' he said quickly. 'I'd drive you myself, but that wouldn't be fair. You need time alone with Tom.'

'Very well. I'll arrange it with his housemaster.'

'Not the one who fancies you?'

'The very same.' She smiled cheekily. 'Goodnight, Joss.'

For a moment she was sure he was about to kiss her, then the memory of the evening before obviously deterred him, and he picked up her hand and kissed her fingers instead.

'Goodnight, Lucy. Sleep well.'

Which was a nice thought, Lucy mused as she undressed, but unlikely after such a momentous evening. The thought of the coming week filled her with misgivings. It would be difficult, to say the least, to live under the same roof as a man who'd just asked her to marry him, when she couldn't even give him an official answer until she'd consulted with her son!

Just before sleep finally overtook her, a thought swam to the surface in Lucy's mind, depressing in its clarity. If she didn't marry Joss, would he still let her have the money as a loan?

When Lucy went down to breakfast next morning, dressed rather more elegantly than usual for the shop, only one place was laid at table. To her annoyance, she felt oddly let down.

'Only me this morning, Mrs B?'

'Yes, dear.' Mrs Benson put down a fresh pot of coffee and took an envelope from the pocket of her overall. 'Mr Joss left this note for you. Now, let me cook you something nice instead of just toast.'

It took some time to convince Mrs Benson that toast was all she wanted, and Lucy was finally alone. She opened the envelope quickly, needing to read what Joss had written before she felt up to eating anything.

'I'm off to London for a few days to see my publishers and take care of a few things,' Joss's note began. 'It will be easier for you this way, Lucy. Please make yourself at home, ask Mrs Benson for anything you need, and if you don't fancy driving the Land Rover, there's a Volkswagen Polo you can use to get yourself into town every day. I'll see you on Sunday evening when you get back.'

The note was signed with his initial, and Lucy eyed the looped black 'J' pensively. She had geared herself up to a week of evenings spent in Joss's company, and now he'd tactfully taken himself off instead she felt humiliatingly flat. She ate some toast without enthusiasm, drank the entire contents of the coffee-pot, then went in search of Benson, who took her out to the garages at the back of the house to show her the car she was to use.

'Mr Joss thought the Land Rover might be a bit big for you,' said Benson, smiling indulgently.

'This neat little beauty is certainly more my size. Thanks, Benson, see you tonight.' Lucy drove off carefully, her mind working at a furious state as she accustomed herself to the strange car. If she decided to change her mind, go back home, or even move in over the shop, this was the perfect opportunity. There was nothing to stop her now Joss had taken himself off. Was he *that* confident of her consent? Perhaps he considered Tom's agreement a mere formality. Not that she could return to Holly Lodge in its present condition, of course, nor was there much hope of moving into the flat, either, until certain basic improvements had been added—like a bathroom and a kitchen, for starters. Very probably Mr Jonas Woodbridge was well aware of all this. Lucy sighed as she reached the outskirts of Abbotsbridge, negotiating the borrowed car very carefully through the early morning traffic until she reached the safety of the cobbled courtyard behind the shop. It struck her that, if Tom didn't fancy Joss as a stepfather, these few days of luxury at Abbot's Wood were all she'd know of comfort for some time. The temptation was too strong. Just this little interlude, Lucy pleaded with herself. No meals to cook, no housework to do after her day at the shop; just a very welcome bit of pampering from Mrs Benson, who'd always had a soft spot for young Lucy Drummond.

Lucy unlocked the shop, then rang Perdy to say she wasn't needed that afternoon, but if she could tear herself away from the new man's arms for an hour Lucy would buy her a pub lunch and tell her about the happenings of the last day or two. Not everything, thought Lucy. The marriage proposal was a private thing. But, since the entire town probably knew she was staying at Abbot's Wood by now, it was only fair to tell Perdy herself rather than have her friend learn about it second-hand. And, having taken rather more pains with her appearance that morning, for reasons she preferred to ignore, Lucy found the idea of going out for a meal rather nice. She'd have to watch herself, she thought, as she rearranged some ornaments on the Pembroke table in the shop window. Just because

Joss had taken her out for dinner the evening before, there was no reason for her to make a habit of such luxuries.

Perdita Roche arrived dead on one, every red hair gleaming, her freckled nose literally quivering with curiosity at the prospect of Lucy's news. She breezed into the shop in a swirl of green wool cloak, her cat's eyes brimming with mischief.

'And what have you been up to, then, Lucy Drummond? Tell Auntie *all* immediately!'

'Not immediately,' said Lucy firmly. 'Let's get to the Drover's Arms first. I'm starving.' And Perdy had to possess her soul in patience until they were tucked away in a corner of the bar, with glasses of lager and a couple of home-made meat pies steaming in front of them before Lucy began on her story.

Perdy listened, wide-eyed, to the story of the drive home, the accident in the car, the damage to Holly Lodge, but when Lucy came to the bit where Joss Woodbridge arrived on the scene Perdy almost choked on a mouthful of pie.

'Good grief,' she said, when she'd stopped coughing. 'I thought you never let him darken your door, Lucy.'

'I didn't have much choice—the wretched thing was open. Anyway,' went on Lucy, suddenly very busy with her pie, 'he insisted I spend the night at Abbot's Wood after I found you weren't home.'

Perdy regarded Lucy's carefully blank face with suspicion. 'And you went? Without a struggle?'

'I argued a bit.' Lucy's cheeks warmed, and she swallowed some lager. 'But it was very late, and cold, and somehow it seemed the only sensible thing to do.'

'And was the offer for a share of *his* bed?'

'Of course not! Mrs Benson installed me in a very comfortable guest-room, nosy.'

'Oh, yes, the Bensons. I'd forgotten about them.' Perdy jumped up and went to the bar for coffees. When she got back, she had the air of someone set on learning every last detail. 'So what's happening now, then, Lucy? How the dickens are you going to pay for all the repairs—since I assume you never managed to keep up both insurance premiums?'

'You presume right. And it's going to be pretty difficult, but I'll find a way.' Lucy didn't elaborate on the exact nature of the way she was contemplating, but set Perdy gaping again by telling her Abbot's Wood was to be Lucy Drummond's address until the end of the week.'

'Goodness! Will Holly Lodge be OK by then?'

Lucy nodded vaguely and changed the subject by asking about Perdy's new boyfriend. Nothing loth, her friend plunged into a glowing account of Paul Manning, an artist and gorgeous with it, with a lovely silky beard and a talent for cooking.

'*Very* useful.' Lucy grinned mischievously. 'At least you'll be fed as well as bedded while he's here.'

'How do you know I'm being "bedded" as you so delicately put it?' Perdy tried to look indignant, but dissolved into giggles as Lucy told her bluntly it was obvious.

'You glow, Perdita Roche. You glow!'

Perdy sobered, and reached across to take Lucy's hand. 'You could do with a bit of glow yourself, Lucy, love. Those big brown eyes look very strained.'

'Since the particular glow in question is taboo in Abbotsbridge for single ladies with ten-year-old sons, I'll just have to keep my worry-lines.' Lucy patted Perdy's long, capable hand. 'You enjoy your Paul, darling, and don't worry about me. Things have a way of working out.'

It was something Lucy assured herself a great deal over the next few days. Her daily visits to the lodge depressed her utterly, even though the house was drying out a little owing to a welcome change in the weather. Spring, it seemed, had finally decided to put in an appearance, but the sunshine only showed up all the wear and tear in the small house with unremitting cruelty.

'You sound depressed,' said Joss, when he rang up half-way through the week.

'Guilty, rather than depressed, because I feel I've no right to be here sitting by your fire, watching your television and eating a delicious dinner on a tray in sinful comfort.'

'Why on a tray?'

'Mrs Benson had every intention of serving me in state in the dining-room.' Lucy chuckled. 'This was the compromise, since both Bensons were most put out by my suggestion of eating in the kitchen. I don't know why—I used to run in and out of it often enough with Simon.'

'I remember.' Joss sounded distant. 'How are the repairs going at your place?'

'Very well. It's in a terrible mess at the moment, with pipes everywhere and sawdust all over the place from the new floorboards, but I've put dust sheets in all the rooms.' She paused. 'Thank you for organising it, Joss.'

'Don't thank me. Thank Ted.' He changed the

subject. 'Have you contacted the school?

'Yes. I'm taking Tom out for lunch on Sunday, but he wants to be back in school early. Some special film show. I should be back here by six at the latest.'

'Good. I'll be waiting. Goodnight, Lucy.'

The week went by with surprising speed. The spring sunshine brought more people out than usual. The majority of those who visited the shop came to look rather than buy, but there was a feeling of bustle and activity in the air that had been missing during the period since Christmas. Perdy helped out on the Saturday, and Lucy took advantage of her presence to get her hair trimmed and washed in the lunch hour.

'I hope Tom appreciates his mother's efforts.' Perdy eyed Lucy's elegant, curly head afterwards, her eyebrows shooting up as Lucy displayed the contents of a bag bearing the name of Abbotsbridge's most fashionable dress shop.

'I haven't had anything new for ages,' said Lucy defensively, as Perdy admired the jacket and skirt in damson red wool. 'I thought Tom deserved a well-dressed mother for a change.'

'I'm sure *Tom* will be most impressed,' said Perdy, poker-faced. 'But I thought you were broke.'

'I am. I used my credit card, much against my principles.' Lucy shrugged. 'Perhaps I'll have sold the house by the time I have to pay if off.'

Perdy's vivid face softened. 'I hope so, love. Anyway, I sold that pair of stone vases this morning to Mrs Hope-Seddon. She fancied something genuinely antique to grow her geraniums in this year. I'm afraid she knocked me down to a hundred and fifty pounds, though.'

Lucy's eyes goggled. 'But they were only a hundred for the pair!'

Perdy clapped a hand to her mouth. 'Oh, crumbs—I thought that was *each*, Lucy!' She began to giggle. 'The old dragon was frightfully pleased, anyway, and God knows she can afford it.'

'I should tell her——' began Lucy, but Perdy interrupted fiercely.

'No, you won't. If you insist, I'll refund her money myself. But my advice is to put it towards your new suit.'

Any guilt Lucy felt about Perdy's transaction disappeared when Tom dashed out of school next day, full of approval for her appearance.

'Gosh, you look great! Is that new?' He waved a brown paw at her outfit, his own appearance far from well groomed, despite his grey flannel Sunday suit.

Lucy resisted the urge to straighten his tie and smooth the unruly dark curls. 'Yes. Like it?'

Tom nodded enthusiastically as they made for the car park near the cricket pitch. 'Why are you taking me out?' he demanded. 'Worsley and Bannister are pretty fed up about it. You weren't supposed to come until *exeat*.'

Lucy braced herself. 'Yes, I know. But there's something we have to talk over, Tom. Over lunch,' she added firmly, and her son brightened.

'Where?'

'I thought that nice pub down by the river.'

Tom's eyes glistened. *'Great!'* He scanned the cars in the car park. 'Where's the car?'

'I crashed it, remember? I wrote to you about it.'

Tom looked guilty. 'Oh, crikey, I forgot! Sorry, Mother—are you OK?' He examined Lucy anxiously from head to toe for visible injuries.

'I'm fine.' Lucy led the way to the yellow Polo, and Tom whistled.

'It's brand new,' he breathed in awe. 'Where did you get it?'

'I borrowed it.' Lucy got in and opened the passenger door for Tom, who was loud with admiration for the radio and cassette player until he saw the selection of tapes.

'No pop?' he asked in disgust.

'No, you savage. Listen to the radio instead.'

Tom's pleasure in the inn's excellent lunch was so great that Lucy left any serious discussion until he'd dispatched his portion of apple pie and cleared up most of her cheese after it. Finally, she had no option but to mention the reason for her visit.

'Tom, I've got a few questions to ask, and I'd like you to answer them truthfully,' Lucy began. 'Don't tell me what you think I want to know. I need honesty.'

Tom eyed her apprehensively. 'OK.'

Lucy frowned, trying to find the right words. 'It's quite a time now since you first met Mr Woodbridge.'

Tom looked blank. 'Mr Woodbridge?'

'Yes. I'd rather like to know how you feel about him.'

Tom was plainly taken aback. 'I—I like him. He's great. He doesn't talk sort of silly.'

'How do you mean?'

'Well, not like Mr Fenton.'

Eric Fenton, the curate of St Mary's Church in

Abbotsbridge, squired Lucy to local concerts very
occasionally. A bachelor, he had an uneasily hearty
manner in his dealings with Tom.

'How does Mr Woodbridge talk to you, then?'

'Same as Gramp did,' said Tom gruffly, and
Lucy nodded, enlightened. Her father had treated
Tom like a contemporary.

'So you get on with him quite well, then?'

'I don't see him that much, do I?' Tom looked
uncomfortable and gazed through the window. 'I
know you're not keen on me going to Abbot's
Wood. Gramp said it was because you and Joss
had a bit of a barney once.'

Joss? Lucy made a note of that. 'True. We did.
He—he made me very angry.'

'But Gramp said Joss tried to apologise lots of
times afterwards, and you wouldn't listen.' Tom
turned to look at her. Accusingly, Lucy saw, with a
pang. 'Gramp said it was over—over his brother.'
His eyes dropped.

'That's right,' said Lucy, her heart constricting.
Poor Tom. He never questioned his parentage. At
least, not to her. She knew very well that Tom had
taken his queries on the subject to her father, and
whatever that forceful gentleman had seen fit to
tell his grandson had seemed to satisfy him up to
the present. It seemed fairly certain Tom knew
Simon Woodbridge of Abbot's Wood was his
father. That he never taxed his mother with it was a
credit to the upbringing instilled in him by his
grandfather.

'The thing is, Tom,' Lucy went on, trying to be
honest, 'people say some pretty hurtful things
when they're crazy with grief. And Mr
Woodbridge was in a terrible state about Simon's

death, and thought I was to blame.'

'You weren't, were you?' Tom looked anxious.

Lucy explained quickly about the illicit flying lessons, and how Joss thought she should have let him know about them. Tom's face cleared.

'Well, you couldn't sneak, could you?'

Lucy sighed. 'No. But afterwards I wished I had.'

Tom nodded sympathetically, looking touchingly mature in his desire to comfort. 'But Joss isn't mad at you any more, is he?'

'No.'

'Are you still mad at him?'

Lucy paused. 'No.' she said slowly. 'No, I'm not. In fact, Tom . . .' She took a deep breath. 'What would you say if I told you Mr Woodbridge wants to marry me?'

Tom's eyes were like saucers. 'You mean, you'd be *Mrs* Woodbridge?'

Lucy blinked, eying him warily. 'Well, yes, I'd have to be, wouldn't I?'

'And Joss would be my stepfather, and come to the First Eleven matches and speech day and——'

'Tom!' Lucy cut through the outpourings, the wind taken out of her sails completely. 'Do I take it you approve?'

'*Do* I!' For a moment Lucy thought her son would actually forget himself entirely and embrace her in public, but he subsided sheepishly and grinned at her. 'Fantastic!' he said simply.

CHAPTER FIVE

LUCY was prey to a variety of emotions as she drove back through the sunny, mild afternoon. It was fortunate that the weather was vastly different from her previous journey, since her concentration was on the talk with Tom, instead of on the road. But by this time she was familiar with the car and drove automatically, thinking of Tom's obvious pleasure at the prospect of Joss as his stepfather. Lucy had not been prepared for such wholehearted approval from her son. She had, she realised, been ready to coax a little, if necessary, which was revealing. Tom wasn't the only one, it seemed, who fancied the idea of the proposed marriage. His mother wasn't nearly as averse to it as she had tried to make herself believe.

Several miles passed in self-analysis as Lucy came to the conclusion that her bitterness towards Joss Woodbridge all these years had been in the nature of a barrier constructed to conceal and contain her desperate hurt. She had a suspicion that her refusal to see Joss every time he came to apologise had been because the barrier would probably have crumbled away if they'd met face to face. Her father had unflaggingly tried to make peace between his daughter and Jonas Woodbridge, but Lucy wasn't 'Bulldog' Drummond's daughter for nothing.

As Lucy turned the Volkswagen up the drive to

Abbot's Wood she felt tense, wishing she could turn tail and run away. Which was very similar to the way she'd felt when she'd found she was pregnant. And if she could stand her ground and face up to *that* little problem at the tender age of seventeen, it was surely possible to cope with the coming interview with Joss now she was so much older and wiser. Wiser? Lucy's laugh was derisive as she parked the car in front of the house. Before she could even switch off the ignition the wide door was thrown open and Joss came out to help her from the car. He looked tired. Some of his tan had faded, and his formal dark suit made him look older, more remote.

'Hello, Lucy.' He took her arm and led her indoors. 'How's Tom?'

'Fine.'

'Let's have a drink.' A vein was throbbing in his temple, Lucy saw, and she relaxed. His tension somehow lessened hers. His feeling for Tom obviously ran very deep, she thought, as she watched him pouring the drinks once they were in the study.

'Thank you, Joss.' Lucy accepted the whisky and soda gratefully. 'How was your trip to London?'

'Hectic.' Joss swallowed half his drink, then sat down, eyeing her. 'You look very elegant, Lucy.'

She smiled. 'It's difficult trying to maintain a balance when I visit Tom. The aim is to look good but not different. Of course, with enough money, or breeding, one can get away with darned sweaters and manure-smeared breeches, like the mother of Tom's bosom pal Bannister. But she's the daughter of "a lord or something", to quote my son.'

Joss smiled sardonically. 'Does all this determined small talk mean I'm about to get the thumbs down?'

'Quite the reverse. Tom was surprisingly enthusiastic about having you for a stepfather.'

Something leapt in Joss's eyes. 'He *was*?'

'Oh, yes. Quite ecstatic about having a mother called Mrs Woodbridge.' Lucy's smile was bleak. 'Until that moment, Tom had never let on that it troubled him to have Miss Drummond for a mother.'

Very gently Joss drew her up out of her chair, as if she were spun glass and likely to shatter at his touch. Lucy leaned against him, suddenly glad of his support, glad of someone to share this moment with her.

'Once the main issue had been tackled,' she said wearily, 'I plucked up enough courage to ask Tom if he'd always minded about my not being married, and he said Gramp had explained it all, told him Simon had been killed in an accident, which was why marriage wasn't possible.' Lucy felt Joss's arm tighten about her. 'Apparently Dad explained that babies happened sometimes when two people weren't married, especially when they were fond of each other.' A tremor ran through her. 'So really the only reassurance Tom seemed to need was that I *had* been fond of Simon. And since, God knows, I was, that seemed to be that.'

Joss tipped her head back to look down into her face. 'Do you still love Simon, Lucy?'

'It's eleven years since he died, Joss. All I have now is the memory of how I felt about him. I was only seventeen, for pity's sake.' Lucy's eyes darkened. 'Surely you don't expect me to be faithful to a memory for the rest of my life!'

'On the contrary.' His smile was wry. 'If you do agree to marry me, I would much prefer a wife not wholly given over to memories of another man. Even if the man was my brother.'

Lucy stepped back. 'Right. Then that's all cleared up, isn't it? All neat and tidy.'

'You don't sound over-enthusiastic.' Joss poured himself another drink, looking morose. 'Is the thought of marrying me so depressing?'

Lucy felt contrite. 'No, of course not. I'm sorry, Joss, but it's been a rather unsettling sort of day.'

'Amen to that.' Joss tossed back the drink in one swallow. 'Let's start again, then, shall we? Pretend I've just gained the more conventional form of consent for your hand.'

'From my father, you mean, instead of my son?' She grinned, and Joss's eyes lit with warmth.

'Exactly. I think your father would have approved.'

'I agree. He thought a lot of you. It used to annoy him intensely when I—I——'

'Refused to agree with him?' Joss smiled crookedly. 'I know. He told me as much.'

Lucy spread her hands. 'So. Now you're quite sure of full approval, father and son——'

'I think it's time I now asked *you* if you'll marry me. Not Tom Drummond Senior's daughter, nor Tom Drummond Junior's mother, but you, Lucy.' Joss's eyes held hers very steadily. 'Are you willing to be my wife?'

'Yes, Joss.' She hesitated. 'But with certain conditions.'

His eyes narrowed. 'Conditions? I thought I was being reasonably accommodating already.'

'Yes, of course you are. And I'm very grateful,
truly I am.' Lucy's eyes filled with pleading. 'But
I'm not sure I'm ready to be a wife yet in all the
ways you naturally expect.'

'Don't wrap it up, Lucy.' His voice cut like a
blade. 'You mean you don't relish the thought of
my conjugal demands.'

'I didn't mean it quite like that,' she said, stung.
'But please try to understand. For years I've
thought of you as the enemy——'

'Don't I know it!'

'Well, I can't pretend, Joss. I'll admit it's some
time since I've felt the same hurt and—and
resentment I did at first, but when I have thought
of you it hasn't been with warmth. So all I'm
asking is that you give me time. Time to get used to
the idea of you as a husband.' Lucy wished she'd
never broached the subject. Joss looked
frighteningly cold. She'd been stupid not to
anticipate his reaction. 'If you feel strongly on the
subject, of course, I do understand.' she went on
awkwardly, quailing at the look on his face. 'I
mean, you're laying out a lot of money on my
behalf; it's only natural to expect some kind of
return . . .' She trailed into silence at the blaze of
distaste in Joss's eyes.

'If I wanted to buy sex, Lucy,' he said
deliberately, 'I could do so for a lot less than the
sum necessary to put your house in order. Let's get
things straight. I'm marrying you to get Tom. If
you fancied making the marriage the usual, normal
arrangement, fine. But the doubtful boon of your
favours in return for money expended isn't over-
stimulating to my particular libido. I'll keep to *my*
bed and you can keep to yours.' His smile was a

mere glint of white teeth. 'If you change your mind at any time, of course, please let me know and I'll be happy to oblige. Until then, sleep in peace.'

The last words sounded too like something off a tombstone for Lucy's liking, and she shivered. She had put her foot in it, good and proper; touched her future husband on the raw. She looked down at the carpet, then up at Joss.

'What shall I do now?' she asked awkwardly. 'Shall I take myself off to bed, out of your way?'

Joss's face softened. 'Of course not, Lucy. Mrs Benson's left a cold meal waiting in the dining-room. You must be hungry.'

To her surprise, Lucy found she was. Confronted with a large platter of sliced chicken breast garnished with avocado slices and apricots, she was only too ready to enjoy it. She served them both with generous helpings and began to eat with relish.

'I seem to possess a very odd sort of appetite,' Lucy informed him between mouthfuls. 'I couldn't manage much at all lunch time, because of what I had to say to Tom. Yet tonight, even after a disagreement with you, I'm starving.'

Joss unbent enough to chuckle, and began to eat with similar enthusiasm. 'I'm glad. Frankly, you look as though some decent meals wouldn't come amiss. I prefer you as you used to be, Lucy, more rounded.'

Lucy pulled a face. 'Chubby, you mean! I hated it. I was consumed with envy for Caroline's figure.'

'While she, you might like to know, would have given her eye-teeth for your vital statistics in *one* area.'

'You've got to be kidding!'

Joss grinned widely and shook his head. 'No. I distinctly remember Caroline's scorn when she told me that all men went ape over breasts like yours—which meant she envied them like hell.'

Lucy busied herself with her chicken, her cheeks hot. 'Aren't people peculiar?' she said lightly. 'We all want whatever it is we don't have.'

'How true, Lucy.' Joss's smile was wry. 'How very true. Tell me,' he went on casually, 'have you any preference regarding the wedding?'

Lucy paused, fork half-way to her mouth, and put it down again. The wedding ceremony itself was something she hadn't allowed herself to think about yet. 'Oh, something very quiet, under the circumstances. I'm not exactly eligible for white satin and orange blossom, am I!'

Joss's face went rigid. 'Does that trouble you?'

'Since you mention it, no. But I do think we should tie the knot with as little fuss as possible.'

'I disagree,' said Joss forcefully. 'We're both residents of this parish, so I suggest we get married in St Mary's Church in Abbotsbridge in the conventional way.'

Lucy stared at him in astonishment. 'With my track record, wouldn't a Register Office be more suitable?'

Joss jumped up and came round the table, putting a finger under her chin to tilt her face to his. 'But that's the whole point of the exercise, Lucy. I want a public demonstration to show Abbotsbridge that Lucy Drummond's name will be Woodbridge at last, as it should have been for the past eleven years, with as many people present as possible to witness the ceremony.' He smiled bleakly. 'At least the name's the same, even if I'm not the bridegroom you originally wanted.'

Lucy opened her mouth to contradict him, then thought better of it. 'I don't need all that, Joss!'

He shrugged and returned to his place. 'Personally, I think it's the best way.'

They went on arguing about the ceremony for the remainder of the meal, and even once they were back in the study, but Joss was adamant.

'Six weeks should do to get you used to the whole idea and let me get some work done on the book, so let's say the last Saturday in April, just before Tom goes back to school. That should fit in all round.' Joss smiled suddenly. 'Unless of course, you had some idea of Tom coming with us on our honeymoon?'

'Lord, no!' Lucy eyed him warily. 'Is a honeymoon strictly necessary, Joss?'

'Absolutely.' Joss lit a cigar. 'Besides, you told me you had a yen for places with strange-sounding names.'

'Well, yes, but under the circumstances——'

'A couple of weeks in different surroundings will help you adjust to our marriage far more easily than merely moving along the gallery here from your room to mine.' His eyes were very steady as they held hers. 'Perhaps I should make it clear right now that I want you to share my room, Lucy, even if you sleep alone in the bed'.

'Where will you sleep then?'

'There's a couch in my dressing-room.'

'But you can't sleep there indefinitely!'

'I don't intend to.' Joss smiled into her startled eyes through a cloud of smoke. 'I meant you won't be afflicted with my company *all* that long, Lucy.

I'm off to Brazil later on in the summer,
remember.'

'As soon as that?'

'As soon as the present book's finished, at least.'
Joss tapped his ash into the fire. 'So you won't
have to put up with too much of my company.
You'll be a grass widow far more than a wife.'

Later, when she was alone in the privacy of the
guest-room, Lucy began to regret making such a
noise about the sexual side of marriage to Joss.
Only days before she had been reviling fate for her
single, ambiguous status, yet given the wholly
unexpected opportunity to change it she had
behaved like a prudish ninny. She sighed. When it
came to Joss Woodbridge, her common sense
seemed to go walkabout! Lucy scowled at her
reflection as she slapped cleansing cream on her
face, gloomily eyeing the clear-cut features that
looked so good on the men of the Drummond
family. For a woman they were a shade too
strongly marked for any pretensions to beauty,
particularly the nose. She turned away impatiently
and tissued her face clean, then slumped on the
stool in front of the dressing-table. If only she
could go back to Holly Lodge. Perhaps it would be
easier to cope with this disturbing prospect of
marriage if she could grow used to it by degrees.
With sudden purpose, Lucy jumped up and pulled
on her dressing-gown, then went out along the
gallery to Joss's room and knocked.

Joss opened the door and looked at her with
raised eyebrows. 'Something wrong?'

He was still partly dressed, in white shirt and
dark trousers, his feet bare. He had very nice toes,
Lucy noticed irrelevantly. 'No, nothing wrong,

exactly, Joss. Could I come in for a moment?'

'Of course.' Joss held open the door for her and waved a hand towards a tapestry chair near one of the windows. Lucy sat down, fiddling with the sash of her dressing-gown. She glanced at the large, tester bed, then looked away again quickly.

'Come to inspect your future quarters?' asked Joss suavely.

'No.' Lucy refused to rise to the mockery in his voice. 'Joss, I came to say I think I should go back home to live until—until the wedding.'

He frowned. 'Surely it isn't even habitable yet, Lucy. Is that sensible?'

'Only the landing and hall are in a real mess. The plumber has finished with the piping, so I see no reason why I can't go home in the evenings. The electricity's back on, and I can light fires to dry the place out properly, switch on my electric blanket.' Lucy looked at him squarely. 'This way, everything will be easier. I can get used to the idea of marrying you more gradually.'

'Which you find difficult while you're living here, I take it?' Joss didn't move a muscle, but something told Lucy plainly he wasn't as calm as he looked.

'It's an unnatural situation,' she said flatly. 'You must see that. But if you, well, come round and visit me now and then, even take me out occasionally, it would seem more normal—more like other people's arrangements.'

A gleam of amusement lit Joss's blue eyes as he leaned indolently against one of the bedposts. 'Lucy Drummond—are you by any chance asking me to come courting?'

Lucy flushed bright red. 'No, of course not——'

'Because, if so, I think it's a splendid idea.' He stood upright, his teeth showing white in a smile Lucy viewed with misgiving. 'Inspired, in fact. Forgive me for not thinking of it myself. You never had much real courtship from Simon, did you?'

'Joss, that's not quite what I meant!' Lucy got up, flustered, and made for the door, but he barred her way, grasping her gently by the upper arms.

'I'll go round to your place after you've left for the shop in the morning, Lucy, see how things are first. If the house is half-way reasonable, I'll see it's made habitable by tomorrow evening.'

'Thank you,' she said quietly. 'I'm sure it's better this way—easier all round.'

'And will it give you time to steel yourself to becoming my wife?' His eyes mocked her.

'Yes. It will. One can't swing from one extreme to the other overnight.' She smiled crookedly. 'I never really thought I'd marry anyone, you know. Ever.'

'And no doubt the last person you'd have expected to marry was me!'

'Exactly.'

Blue eyes stared intently into brown in silence, then Joss released her and stepped back. 'So, goodnight once more, Lucy.'

'Goodnight—and thank you.' Lucy held out her hand as though they were sealing a bargain, and Joss took it in his and held it.

'Since I somehow feel we've just become formally betrothed,' he said softly, 'would it be infringing on any of your rules to request a kiss in honour of the occasion?'

A smile lit Lucy's dark eyes. 'Couched in such terms, how can I refuse?' She held up her face, eyes closed, then opened them again to see Joss's face very close to hers. The unguarded look of heat in his eyes took her by surprise. Her own widened and her lips parted and Joss bent to kiss them, in a way that unsettled her so much, she rocked on her heels and grabbed at his arms to steady herself. After which there seemed little point in complaining when Joss put those same arms round her and held her tightly while he kissed her again, with such unhurried savour Lucy relaxed and abandoned herself to the pleasure of the moment. When Joss lifted his head at last, the sleepy look in his long blue eyes sent trickles of response skimming down her spine. She stepped back, retreating from an embrace that had become too pleasurable for her own peace of mind. Lucy cleared her throat, gave Joss a startled smile and said goodnight.

'Shall I take you back to your room, Lucy?' He brushed a hand over her ruffled curls.

Lucy's smile widened a little. 'No. I'll manage to get myself back quite safely, thank you.' Rather more safely, I think, than if you escorted me, she thought as she went back along the gallery.

As Lucy got into bed she was more than a little fed up with herself. What an idiot she had been to shy at sharing Joss's bed! The way she felt right now, it seemed a very, very attractive prospect. Which only showed what a shallow, superficial sort of creature she must really be, since it was only a very short time since Jonas Woodbridge had been the object of her undying displeasure, and had figured, to quote his own words, as villain of the piece in the Lucy Drummond story. Ah! said a nasty little voice in her head, but you know love is said to be the reverse side of hate, Lucy.

That, of course, was impossible. He was still the same Jonas Woodbridge; a fact which it might be as well to remember, even if Tom was thrilled to have him for a stepfather. Which was the object of the exercise, she reminded herself, and something Joss could hardly achieve without marrying Tom's mother. She was a sort of unavoidable extra.

Lucy's sense of fair play rose up in protest at the last bit. That was going too far. Perhaps her grudge had been nurtured too long, and it was time to bury the hatchet. Simon would have been pleased, that was certain. Which thought reassured Lucy so much, she fell asleep thinking it.

CHAPTER SIX

IN THE morning, Joss was missing from the breakfast table, but Lucy found a note on her plate, telling her to borrow the Volkswagen and meet him at Holly Lodge when she closed the shop for the day.

Lucy felt a lot lighter of heart on this particular Monday than she had the week before. Just seven short days earlier all the troubles of the world had seemed a great burden she was obliged to shoulder like Atlas, but now there was light at the end of the tunnel. If occasionally she was visited by the thought that Joss was more or less buying himself a wife and stepson, she dismissed it at once. And when thoughts of that goodnight kiss strayed into her mind far too often, Lucy dismissed those too, even more summarily. Kisses—those sort of kisses —were rare in her experience. Which, no doubt, was why she kept thinking about them. It was the novelty.

Surprisingly, the shop was busy for a Monday. In between her usual Monday chores Lucy sold an art nouveau screen to an elderly lady complaining of draughts in her sitting-room. A Staffordshire stirrup cup in the shape of a fox's head went to a young groom from the local riding stables as a present for her farmer fiancé's birthday, and, flushed with success, Lucy even went so far as to buy a Victorian locket and ear-rings set with seed-pearls and amethysts from a very contemporary young lady.

'My great-aunt left me the hideous things,' said the girl, shuddering. 'Any hope of your taking them off my hands?'

Lucy gave her a fair price, set the pieces aside for cleaning, and prepared to shut up shop for the day. When she arrived at Holly Lodge later, she found it had undergone something of a transformation. All the lights were on, a fire was blazing in the sitting-room, and Joss stood chatting to the men who were putting the carpet down again in the hall.

'Just a temporary arrangement, Lucy,' he said, and came forward to kiss her deliberately, keeping her in the crook of his arm as he turned back to the workmen. 'A new one will be needed, of course, but in the meantime cover this one carefully when you're painting.'

'Right you are, Mr Woodbridge.' They took their leave respectfully, and Lucy gave Joss a wry smile.

'Saving the money on a newspaper announcement?'

He smiled. 'No. I sent an announcement to the papers this morning.'

'Did you now?' Lucy went to the kitchen to put the kettle on, her nostrils twitching at the appetising aroma coming from the Aga. 'Good heavens, Joss, don't say you've cooked dinner, too!'

'Have a heart, I'm not that efficient! In fact, I can't even stay long.'

Lucy felt suddenly flat. 'Going out?' she asked casually, and spooned instant coffee into two mugs.

'I'd already promised to dine with Caroline's

father tonight. I didn't think you'd care to come with me, so I got Mrs Benson to throw a casserole together, and she says you're to eat every bit or she'll be offended.' Joss sat on one of the old Windsor chairs, eyeing her cautiously.

Lucy shook her head at him. 'I managed to take care of myself perfectly well before you took on the job, you know.'

Joss looked unconvinced. 'Let's say since you are now officially my fiancée, Lucy, I prefer to know the house isn't about to fall down about your ears, and a square meal is a certainty, rather than any nonsense about baked beans.'

Lucy's eyes softened. 'Thank you, Joss. I do appreciate it—truly. I just can't get used to it all quite yet, that's all.'

'Perhaps this will help.' Joss reached into his pocket and took out a box, holding it out to her.

Lucy looked at it suspiciously, and Joss got to his feet, opened the box and slid the ring inside on Lucy's finger. She gazed down at it, speechless. A flawless solitaire diamond on a heavy gold band adorned her small, workmanlike hand.

'Well?' he demanded. 'Do you like it?'

Lucy breathed in deeply. 'How could I not? It's —it's quite wonderful.' She looked up at him. 'But, in our case, was it absolutely necessary?'

Joss turned away, an odd look on his face. Was he actually hurt? Lucy wondered.

'I think it's rather more necessary in our case than in the more orthodox type of engagement.' Joss swung back to face her. 'The notice will be in both the local and national papers in the morning, so no doubt all Abbotsbridge will be swarming into the shop to congratulate you. Don't you think they'll expect to see a ring on the appropriate finger?'

'I see. How did you manage to produce one at such short notice? I only agreed last night.'

'I took a chance and bought it in London last week.' He smiled wryly. 'A hostage to fortune, if you like.'

'Oh.' Lucy twisted the ring on her finger. 'What did the announcement say, Joss?'

'Nothing fancy. Something to the effect that a marriage has been arranged between Lucinda Drummond of Holly Lodge, and Jonas Woodbridge of Abbot's Wood, and so on. The date's fixed with the rector, by the way,' he added.

'Really?' Lucy swallowed. Suddenly everything was moving so fast.

'He was very pleased, I might add.'

'Even about me?'

'*Particularly* about you,' said Joss with emphasis. 'He's very happy for you, Lucy.'

'Probably thinks I'm amazingly lucky!' Lucy grinned. 'Which I am, of course. I'm to marry a clever, wealthy, handsome man who intends paying all my debts. How lucky can a girl get?'

Joss took her by the shoulders, shaking her slightly. 'Cut it out, Lucy. I'm gaining at least as much.' He smiled, with a look of such intimacy that bright colour flamed in her cheeks. 'At least I hope to—one day.' And he pulled her close and kissed her in a way intended to clear up any doubt she might have regarding the precise nature of his hopes.

Lucy made no attempt at resistance. With a valuable ring on her finger to underline her indebtedness to Joss Woodbridge even further, it seemed only fair to let him kiss her as much as he liked. And she liked it, too. Her heart was behaving like a wild thing in her chest, in fact, and when Joss raised his head at long last she was breathing as raggedly as he was. He looked down into her dazed, sleepy eyes and chuckled exultantly, then kissed her again. Lucy responded wholeheartedly, her arms going to clasp him closer as their open mouths came together with frankly sensual enjoyment. She felt heat ignite inside her and gasped, her hips pushing against him of their own volition. When she registered the iron hardness encountered there she dodged away, her face hot, but Joss caught her, dragging her back against him, one hand in her hair, the other at the base of her spine, holding her so that she was left in no doubt whatsoever of his desire for her.

What would have happened next if the telephone hadn't interrupted them was something Lucy didn't care to think about afterwards. She tore herself out of Joss's arms and picked up the instrument, her poppy-red face averted as she said a breathless hello.

Perdy's voice enquired if Lucy had run all the way home from town and whether it was possible to come round for a few minutes later. Lucy was only too glad.

'Come and share my dinner. Paul, too, if you like.'

Paul, it seemed, had gone home. Perdy was missing him and had gambled on the fact Lucy would be free.

'Isn't that lucky?' said Lucy brightly as she turned away from the phone. 'Perdy Roche is coming over. Now I can get in with the news before she reads it in the paper tomorrow.'

Joss not only looked amused, he looked maddeningly calm, Lucy saw with displeasure. Just as though he hadn't been on the point of throwing her on the kitchen floor only moments earlier.

'Good.' He shrugged on the jacket he'd discarded at some point. 'My reason for keeping my appointment with Jim Erskine is much the same. I'd prefer to tell him about the wedding myself before he reads the announcement.'

'I remember him well,' said Lucy, once more in possession of her poise. 'He was always very sweet to me.'

'He's never forgiven Caroline for taking off, I'm afraid. Calls her children half-breeds.' He flicked a finger against her flushed cheek. 'There's a fire in your bedroom, by the way, the electric blanket's been on all day, and the ceiling on the landing has been re-plastered. The house isn't exactly elegant again, but at least it's habitable.'

Lucy was touched. 'You've been very kind, Joss.'

'Not always,' he reminded her, and made for the door. 'I put some food in your cupboards, too. I would prefer, if possible, a bride with slightly more meat on her bones.'

Lucy scowled. 'You sound like a farmer at a cattle sale!'

Joss shrugged. 'I can't be clever, wealthy, handsome *and* tactful. You left out the most important bit, Lucy. I'm human, too.'

On the point of making a shrivelling reply, Lucy caught sight of the glittering ring on her finger and simmered down. 'Thank you for the ring, Joss.' She twisted it, frowning. 'I seem to be causing you so much expense——'

'I'll itemise it, if you like, and see you pay me back some day. In kind.' His eyes met hers with deliberate intent, and Lucy caught her breath. 'Goodnight, Lucy. Make sure you lock up securely tonight.'

She resisted the urge to tell him she'd been doing so as a matter of course long before he decided to whip her life into shape. 'Yes, Joss, goodnight, Joss. And please thank Mrs Benson for me.'

By the time Perdy arrived later, Lucy had put potatoes to bake in their jackets and set the table with candles and the wine Joss had provided as accompaniment to Mrs Benson's delicious casserole.

'So what are you celebrating?' demanded Perdy, mouth full. 'Did you sell the William the Fourth chairs?'

'No.' Lucy smiled. 'Try again.'

'You've sold the house, then!'

'No.'

'Am I getting warm, you maddening creature?'

Lucy relented. 'Frankly, Perdy, I don't think you'd guess in a hundred years. I'm getting married.'

Perdy stared at Lucy in dismay. 'Not to Eric Fenton!'

Lucy giggled. 'Why not? Not that it's Eric. Tom would join the Foreign Legion!'

'And of course Tom would have to approve.' Perdy's eyes sparkled. 'Come *on,* Lucy. Don't keep me in suspense. Who's the lucky man?'

'Jonas Woodbridge.'

Perdy gasped. 'Are you *serious*?'

Lucy nodded matter-of-factly and went on with her dinner.

'But, Lucy, I thought you hated him!'

Lucy shrugged. 'Well, I did. But it seems a bit immature now to have kept *on* hating him all these years. God knows, he's tried hard enough to heal the breach.'

'And succeeded, good and proper, by the sound of it!' Perdy helped herself to more meat. 'Gosh—the shock's made me even hungrier. Did *you* make this, by the way? It's scrumptious.'

'No. Joss brought it, kind courtesy of Mrs Benson.'

'I spoke to her on the phone tonight, thinking you'd be there.'

'I intended letting you know I was moving back, but I've been quite busy for a Monday.'

Perdy eyed her speculatively. 'Does this mean you'll sell the shop?'

'No fear! Not much point in letting Joss bail me out if——' Lucy stopped, and Perdy waggled a finger at her, enlightened.

'Oh, I see, I see. He foots your bills, and in return he gets your body——'

'*And* my son.' Lucy smiled. 'Tom's the big attraction, you know. I'm sure if Joss could get him any other way he would. But whither Tom goes, there go I. *Pro tem*, at least.'

'But he *is* Tom's uncle, in actual fact, darling.'

'Neither officially nor legally, he's not! I have never once made any claim of any kind.'

'You don't have to. Tom's a lot like Simon at the same age.'

'Nonsense. He looks like me.'

Perdy looked unconvinced, but conceded

Harlequin's

Best Ever "Get Acquainted" Offer

Look what we'd give to hear from you

GET ALL YOU ARE ENTITLED TO—AFFIX STICKER TO RETURN CARD—MAIL TODAY

This is our most fabulous offer ever...

AND THERE'S STILL MORE INSIDE.

Let's get acquainted. Let's become friends—

Look what we've got for you:

Get 4 FREE full-length Harlequin Presents® novels.

Plus this lovely lucite clock/ calendar

Plus a surprise free gift

▼ PLUS LOTS MORE! MAIL THIS CARD TODAY ▼

Harlequin's Best-Ever "Get Acquainted" Offer

Yes, I'll try the Harlequin Reader Service® under the terms outlined on the opposite page. Send me 4 free Harlequin Presents® novels, a free digital clock/ calendar and a free mystery gift.

108 CIH CAN2

PLACE STICKER FOR 6 FREE GIFTS HERE

NAME _____

ADDRESS _____ APT. ____

CITY _____

STATE _____ ZIP CODE _____

PRINTED IN U.S.A.

Don't forget...

...Return this card today and receive 4 free books, free digital clock/calendar and free mystery gift.

...You will receive books before they're available in stores and at a discount off the cover prices.

...No obligation to buy. You can cancel at any time by writing "cancel" on your statement or returning a shipment to us at our cost.

If offer card is missing, write to: Harlequin Reader Service,
901 Fuhrmann Blvd., P.O. Box 1867, Buffalo, N.Y. 14269-1867

BUSINESS REPLY CARD

First Class   Permit No. 717   Buffalo, NY

Postage will be paid by addressee

Harlequin Reader Service®
901 Fuhrmann Blvd.
P.O. Box 1867
Buffalo, NY 14240-9952

No Postage
Necessary
If Mailed
In The
United States

gracefully and took Lucy's lead, talking about Paul for the rest of the evening. When it was time to go she kissed Lucy, by no means a normal habit of hers. 'I'm glad for you, Lucy. Really glad. Be happy.'

'I'll try.' Lucy clapped a hand to her forehead. 'Heavens, I forgot! I've got something to show you.' And she ran to the bread bin, where she'd hidden the little leather box in a bread wrapper. She slid the ring on her finger and waved her hand at Perdy. 'There. What do you think of that?'

Perdy stared, then let out a long whistle. 'Honest to God, Lucy, you're on your own! You're given a fantastic rock like that and just forget about it?'

'I was afraid to harm it while I fiddled about with the Aga.' Lucy twisted the ring on her finger. 'Joss thought I ought to wear it tomorrow, in case people read the announcement in the paper and come to the shop out of curiosity.'

'Wear it all the time, Lucy. I think that's what Joss had in mind.' Perdy's tone was dry.

'It doesn't seem right, somehow. I mean, the whole thing's more like a business transaction. No romance, or anything.'

'Well, all I can say, angel, is that if you hear of anyone with a similar business arrangement in mind, remember little Perdita, won't you?'

Joss's prediction proved accurate. The whole of Abbotsbridge, it seemed, ingested the wedding announcement along with their morning tea. By midday, Lucy's nerves were jangling in concert with the bell as people came in pretending to browse, some of those who knew her better not even pretending interest in anything but the ring

on her finger. Most of the reaction was kind, some
of it a little saccharine, but a few comments were
frankly barbed. The common denominator of it all
was that Abbotsbridge en masse considered Lucy
very fortunate. As one old schoolfriend pointed
out, it wasn't every man who fancied marrying
someone in Lucy's particular situation.

Lucy pinned a smile on her lips and prayed for
lunch time, never more thankful in her life to hear
one o'clock chime from the selection of clocks
dotted round the shop. Right on cue, the familiar
Land Rover drew up outside and Joss jumped out,
looking irritatingly marvellous in old brown cords
and a shabby waxed jacket. There seemed to be far
more people in Priory Street than usual, Lucy
noted, as he strode into the shop and kissed her
soundly.

'Come on, then, Lucy. Let's see what the
Drover's Arms has on offer for lunch.'

'On, no, Joss, I don't think I'm up to it. It's
been mayhem in here all morning.' She looked up
at him pleadingly. 'I was going to shut up shop and
collapse with a cheese roll in the office.'

He shook his head. 'Not on your life. Hurry up;
powder your nose or whatever, and come and face
the music.'

Their first public appearance together was by no
means the ordeal Lucy expected. In the pub,
people were full of welcome and congratulations,
but in some clever way Joss saw to it that they were
left in peace to eat their meal.

'There. Not so bad after all, is it?' he said in her
ear.

'I suppose not.' Lucy gave him a sidelong look.
'But I still feel as though I've won first prize at

the cattle show.'

'It'll pass.' Joss laid down his fork and slid an arm behind her along the settle they were sharing. 'For God's sake, Lucy, stop fidgeting. You're like a cat on hot bricks.'

'Take your arm away,' she muttered.

'No, I won't. So relax.'

Lucy gritted her teeth. Joss had always been an overbearing swine, she thought resentfully, then checked herself, remembering she'd do better to forget the past imperfections and try to think of him as her future husband. But it was difficult. 'It's all so unreal, somehow,' she whispered.

'You and me?' said Joss quickly. 'Nevertheless it *is* real, Lucy. You, Tom and I are going to be a family very soon, so you'd better get used to the idea.'

During the weeks that followed Joss took pains to make sure Lucy grew accustomed to her new status. He saw her almost every day, sometimes just for a few minutes, sometimes for an evening, and each Sunday he insisted she spend the entire day at Abbot's Wood. He sent her flowers, brought her books, magazines, chocolates, rang her at all odd moments. He was, she conceded, as assiduous with his attentions as any woman could have wished.

'You don't have to buy me things all the time,' Lucy protested, guilt-ridden at the thought of the money she was costing him. Her debts were paid, the lodge was fresh with new paint, and Joss had insisted on making her a present of the Volkswagen. 'I'm so deep in your debt, it frightens me.'

Joss brushed aside her protest. 'I don't want to

hear about debt between you and me, Lucy. My reasons for sorting out your affairs are not entirely altruistic. Remember what I'm receiving in return!'

'You mean Tom.'

Joss gave her a kindling look, then pulled her into his arms with a new roughness, and kissed her until she was shaking. 'Yes,' he said unevenly, when he raised his head to stare down at her. 'What else could I mean?'

For a week before Tom was due home from school for Easter Lucy hardly saw Joss at all. He was working flat-out on his book. It was going well, apparently, and the efficient lady who transposed his tapes on to the word-processor was working overtime.

'I'd like some free time with Tom when he comes,' said Joss, yawning. It was a Sunday evening and they were lazing in front of the fire with the papers. 'If I get most of it under my belt before next Thursday I can leave the final bit until after the honeymoon.' He glanced at Lucy's fire-flushed face. 'I can do *some* work when we're in Portugal.'

A slight tremor of reaction ran down Lucy's spine at the word 'honeymoon'. She had done her best to put it out of her mind, along with the actual wedding day itself. Sufficient unto the day, had been her motto, and, to be fair, Joss had made no further move to soften her up as far as the physical side was concerned. He kissed her goodnight, took her hand when they went for walks, threw an arm round her shoulders sometimes when they shared a sofa, but otherwise he'd made no attempt to repeat the scene in the kitchen. Lucy hardly knew whether to be glad or sorry, though she couldn't help wondering if his lovemaking had been a direct retaliation to her plea for patience about sharing his bed. Yet Joss had wanted her, all right. Lucy's experience in that particular department was not as varied as Perdy's, she conceded, but nevertheless she had no doubt that Joss's desire for her was very real. And her own reaction, if she were honest, could hardly be described as tepid.

'What time should we be at the school on Thursday?' asked Joss, and Lucy blinked at him owlishly.

'Are you coming with me?'

'Of course. I think Tom might like me to, don't you?'

He would, of course. In fact, Lucy had a fair idea he'd be thrilled to bits. 'Thank you, Joss. That's very good of you.'

'No, it isn't,' he said irritably, then smiled. 'I'm doing myself the favour, not you and Tom. I quite fancy turning up in the good tweed suit to collect my future stepson.' He gave another mammoth yawn, and Lucy got up.

'Time I went, Joss.'

He heaved himself out of the chair, his handsome face apologetic. 'Lord, sorry, Lucy. I'm not very riveting company at the moment. All my energy is channelled into hammering lucid prose out of the notes I scrawled in Fiji. At the moment I'm deep in the pre-colonial struggles for mastery by one Cakombau, ruler of Bau. Quite a character.' He took her hands, smiling down at her. 'And if I dictate far enough into the night, I sleep like the dead instead of getting too excited about our forthcoming nuptials, Lucinda Drummond. Which is why I've been so restrained with you lately. Or hadn't you noticed?'

Lucy shrugged. 'I haven't given it a thought,' she remarked, which was a downright lie.

Joss, by the look in his long blue eyes, knew it. 'Fortunate lady! Untroubled by such base urges. Come on, I'll drive you home.'

Lucy found she was looking forward to Tom's homecoming even more than usual this time. For one thing, it would be so very gratifying to introduce Joss to the headmaster. Jonas Woodbridge was by no means unknown, and it was only human to experience a little spurt of satisfaction at the thought of Tom's pleasure in being able to boast about his new stepfather. Quite a change for him. Not that he ever mentioned any troubles with his contemporaries about his lack of a father, but Lucy knew there were times when he felt it very deeply, just the same.

Joss had settled the question of what to do with Tom during the Easter holiday by taking it for granted the boy would spend his time at Abbot's Wood while his mother was at the shop. Lucy had reservations about it, but decided to leave the subject until Tom came home to decide for himself. She was left in no doubt about his decision, since happiness blazed from his freckled face when he shot out of school just as his mother was being helped down from the Land Rover by Jonas Woodbridge. Lucy swallowed a lump in her throat as Tom suddenly recollected himself enough to slow down as he reached them, allowing Lucy a swift kiss before stretching out his hand formally to Joss.

'Hello, Mother. Hello, Mr Woodbridge.' Tom literally seethed with excitement as he strove to be self-possessed and adult, and only succeeded in looking like an overjoyed little boy. 'It's great of you to come and collect me—gosh, is that a new Land Rover?'

Since Lucy appeared unable to say anything at all, Joss shook Tom's hand gravely and told him he was very pleased to be of help, and yes, the car was new, and once they'd got his gear stowed away in it they would go and look for some lunch. 'Perhaps you'd like to introduce me to your housemaster first,' Joss suggested, with such a sly look at Lucy that her powers of speech were restored.

Tom was only too delighted to introduce Joss to everyone he could think of. Mr Potter, his housemaster, looked a little constrained as the tall, attractive man not only exchanged pleasantries with him, but rather ostentatiously kept Lucy close with one hand while Tom tugged at the other. Joss was obliged to make a tour of inspection of the entire establishment, while Tom buttonholed his friends to meet him, and Lucy was drawn into introductions to other parents, something she had always felt obliged to avoid before.

When the trio took their leave of the headmaster that gentleman was very kind to Lucy, wishing her every happiness when Joss took care to mention the forthcoming wedding.

Tom frowned as he leaned over the back of Lucy's seat when they were finally able to get away.

'What's the matter?' asked Lucy. 'Forgotten something?'

Tom bit his lip, frowning. 'Will I be able to come?'

'Where?'

'To the wedding.'

Joss gave a shout of laughter, and Tom relaxed. 'Of course, you dunce! I'll need you there for support. Weddings are pretty frightening affairs—I'll be scared stiff.'

'Oh, will you?' Lucy eyed him with displeasure. 'And how am I supposed to feel?'

'Thrilled,' said Joss promptly. 'Only for God's sake, no tears. Women always cry buckets at weddings,' he added, for Tom's benefit.

Tom grinned widely. 'No chance. Mother's not the watery sort. Mr Woodbridge——'

'I thought I was Joss!'

The boy looked self-conscious. 'Well, now you and Mother are getting hitched, I wasn't sure what I was to call you.'

'Joss will do very well, I think, don't you?'

From then on Tom was his normal, cheerful self, eating vast quantities of beef and roast potatoes at the Wheatsheaf, and talking away nineteen to the dozen. Any doubts Lucy might still have harboured about marrying Joss vanished as she saw how delighted Tom was with the entire arrangement. But as she watched him chattering to Joss guilt crept in to replace the doubts. If she hadn't been so pig-headed Tom could have enjoyed Joss's company all his life. In which case, she reminded herself, he would have looked on him as an uncle, and the present situation need never have arisen. Joss would never have been obliged to offer marriage to Lucy Drummond to establish a relationship with her son. It was a disquieting thought.

'You're very quiet, Lucy.' Joss was looking at her closely, she realised.

'And how was I supposed to get a word in?' she countered. 'All I've heard is fishing and cricket from you two, with the odd discussion on the Land Rover for variation.'

Tom looked guilty. 'Sorry, Mother. What would you like to talk about?'

Lucy laughed and went on eating her soufflé glacé. 'Oh, just carry on. Don't mind me.'

Tom grinned, then grew thoughtful. 'By the way, I've been wondering, Mother. Are you going to work in the shop after you're married?'

Lucy's eyes flew to Joss's face, which wore a tigerish smile.

'Good question. Are you, Lucy?'

'Well, yes, I suppose so. I hadn't really thought about it.' Which was the truth. Lucy had steadfastly refrained from thinking about life after the wedding. Something in Joss's face made her change the subject hurriedly, and soon afterwards they were making for home, with no need for conversation from either Lucy or Joss on the journey, since Tom's tongue seemed to be hinged at both ends. He chattered away so unflaggingly that Lucy gave Joss a rueful look.

'Time to change your mind, if you like,' she murmured.

He reached out a hand to cover hers as it lay on her knee. 'No chance of that.' He caught Tom's eye, which was noting the caress with interest.

'Bannister said I'd probably get little brothers and sisters now,' Tom observed, 'but I told him he was potty. You're both a bit old, aren't you?'

'Well, thanks a lot!' protested Lucy. 'We're not that ancient, you brat. Anyway, you're quite enough in the way of family for the moment.'

Joss said nothing, and after a swift glance at his shuttered face Lucy changed the subject.

'Mr Potter gave me your report, Tom,' she said with deliberate cruelty, and the awkward moment passed as her son pleaded with her not to open the report just yet. Lucy was relieved to see Joss's spirits restored by the time they arrived at Holly Lodge, and made a mental note to have a talk with Tom on topics one did not discuss without permission. Getting married with a ten-year-old son in attendance seemed likely to be a more ticklish problem than anticipated.

Once Tom's belongings were unloaded, Lucy provided tea and cakes, then rang Perdy, who was holding the fort at the shop.

'Everything all right?' asked Lucy.

'Very nice, actually, love. I've sold two Worcester plates and that lovely Georgian tea-caddy today, plus loads of polish—must be spring-cleaning time. And, best of all, David Rennie from the estate agents left a message. Can he bring some people to look round the house tomorrow?'

Joss poured tea for Lucy when she joined them. 'Good news?' he asked quickly.

She nodded, and told him what Perdy had said, smiling rather ruefully. 'Now it's looking so nice again, I'm a bit sad to see the house go.'

'You don't need it, Lucy.' Joss's eye challenged her. 'Your home—and Tom's—will be at Abbot's Wood soon.' He aimed a playful fist at Tom's chin. 'I'll pick you up in the morning after your mother goes to the shop. You can show me which room you fancy occupying at Abbot's Wood.'

Tom was impressed. 'Can I really choose *any* room?'

'Except the one your mother and I will share.'
Joss's tone was matter-of-fact, and Tom looked at
him for a moment; then, as though some unspoken
agreement had been reached, he nodded.

'OK. Great.' He slid off the chair after
permission from Lucy, whistling as he clattered
upstairs to unpack.

'Which will mean an unholy mess,' said Lucy,
resigned. 'I steel myself not to interfere, except for
his trunk. Everything in that literally leaps out as I
raise the lid—about three days' washing, usually.'

Joss laughed. 'I remember it well. Some of the
sports kit used to come home unwashed from one
half to the next. My aunt used to play merry hell
about the socks, in particular.'

'You were lucky to have someone to deal with
them,' said Lucy with feeling. 'I had to wash my
own stuff.'

Lucy and the Woodbridge boys had possessed,
or rather lacked, one thing in common. They had
all been motherless, Lucy and Simon from birth.
Miss Olivia Woodbridge, their father's sister, had
brought up Joss and Simon, but Bull Drummond
had managed his daughter's upbringing almost
single-handed, with various domestic help. From
time to time he had muttered vaguely about
presenting Lucy with a stepmother, but once she
was old enough to take over the reins of the
household her father had abandoned all pretence
of remarriage and settled comfortably into the
routine he liked best, keeping his social activities
with the opposite sex strictly separate from his life
with Lucy.

'Were you doing a little territorial claim-staking
just now with Tom?' asked Lucy.

'Yes. It's best to let him know where we all stand. And sleep.' Joss's smile was mocking. 'Is the latter still a problem for you?'

Lucy shrugged, unruffled. 'I'm not letting it become one. I'm sure we'll be able to work it out amicably when the time comes.'

Joss's mouth twitched. 'How sensible you are, Lucy!'

Lucy disagreed. 'I think you could describe me as pig-headed, rather than sensible. Dad used to say so, anyway.'

'Since he was cut from the same cloth, I imagine he did. The two of you must have had some fair old arguments in your time.'

'We did. But not over things that really mattered. When Dad learned I was pregnant he was utterly wonderful. No reproaches, no recriminations . . .' Too late, she realised what she was saying.

'Unlike me,' Joss said bitterly.

Lucy jumped to her feet, stricken, and put a hand on his shoulder. 'I wasn't getting at you, Joss. Truly. I spoke without thinking.'

He twisted abruptly, bringing her round to sit on his knee, looking deep into her eyes. 'Do you have any idea how much I hated myself for the things I said to you that day?'

Lucy buried her face on his shoulder. 'Let's not think about—about that any more. Let's wipe the slate clean; go on from here.'

Joss turned her face to his. 'Kiss and be friends, Lucy?'

The look in his eyes was anything but platonic, but she nodded, and he bent his head and kissed her. Her arms stole round his neck and Joss breathed in sharply, his lips parting hers, then a voice said, 'Oh, gosh—sorry!'

They sprang apart, laughing, as Tom eyed them with undisguised interest from the doorway.

'What's the matter?' asked Joss, keeping Lucy on his knee.

Tom rubbed his nose thoughtfully. 'Are you going to do that sort of thing a lot?'

'No more than anyone else.'

'I bet Bannister's parents don't!'

'I'm sure they do,' said Joss emphatically. 'Bannister probably hasn't noticed.'

Tom looked unconvinced, and Lucy slid off Joss's lap. 'Don't worry, Tom, we'll try not to embarrass you too much. Now, I suppose I can't put it off any longer. Where are the keys to that horrible trunk?'

CHAPTER SEVEN

LESS than four weeks later, Lucy Woodbridge found herself following a cobbled road past a monastery and on through tall cypresses which gave shade from the morning sun for a while until gradually the trees thinned out. Joss's hand tightened on hers.

'Not much farther now, Lucy.'

They went on, climbing higher and higher in the warm sunshine, and at last, near the mountain top, they found what he had promised; a dusty track winding through a stand of pines. Stumbling a little in places over the ruts, they followed the path to their goal, which proved to be a high, rocky bluff commanding one of the most spectacular views in Portugal. The sun was hot, but Lucy shivered a little in the cool breeze, and Joss slid an arm round her as they gazed down.

'Awesome,' she said softly.

Joss nodded. 'Easy to see why the spot helped to change the course of European history. This is where Wellington stood in 1810 to direct his army against the French.'

They stood together for a long time, looking down over the sunlit slopes, bound together by a shared sense of history. Afterwards they retraced their steps, and a little way down the mountain went into the military museum to pore over the maps and tableaux, the cannons and muskets and

110

the terrible bayonets that illustrated Joss's remark with such chilling clarity.

'Time to go,' said Joss eventually. 'There's a hundred-mile drive ahead of us, Lucy, so get your skates on.'

'Where now?' Lucy felt she had done more travelling in the past few days than in her entire life previously, and was enjoying herself so much, she forgot for hours at a stretch that this was her honeymoon. No seclusion and romantic lazy hours beside a pool for Mr and Mrs Joss Woodbridge; Joss's way of accustoming Lucy to the idea of marriage was to provide himself with an Audi Avant Quattro car with four-wheel drive that could cope with the most dizzying of twists and turns on a breathtaking tour of most of the scenic delights Portugal could offer, starting on the Portsmouth-Caen ferry, and doing the seven hundred-mile trip to Burgos in one lap.

Lucy had been so tired that first night, she could have shared a room with King Kong for all she cared, and never stirred until a bright and breezy Joss bullied her out of the twin beds next morning so they could go in search of breakfast. The ensuing journey, particularly through the north-east corner of Portugal, had tried Lucy's endurance somewhat, particularly the last tortuous miles to Braganca where they stopped for lunch days later. Lucy had been glad of a walk round the walls of the high, rather lonely city to admire the view back over the wild country they'd just covered, so that her stomach could settle itself sufficiently to enjoy the soup and trout served them at a *pousada* perched on one of the high hills ringing the birthplace of Charles the Second's

queen. By this time, now that the more rigorous
portion of the journey was behind her, Lucy was
almost blasé about the trip to Elvidos, a tiny
mediaeval walled town which had no modern
buildings of any kind, she found, when they
reached it in late afternoon sunshine.

'Oh, Joss, it's lovely, lovely!' She turned ecstatic
dark eyes on her husband.

He smiled. 'I thought we might stay here for a
while, rest a bit and explore the town and the
nearby coast at leisure.'

Lucy assented raptuously, delighted with the
rust-red town walls, the old houses held in close
embrace inside them, and dominating it all the
ancient square castle with its crenellated towers.

'Where are we staying?' By this time, Lucy
found it perfectly natural to share a room with
Joss, though as yet there had never been the
slightest question of sharing a bed, since every
hotel so far had provided them with one each. And
even if they had shared, Lucy thought, both of
them had been so exhausted by their rigorous
travels, sleep would still have been the only thing
on their minds. On hers, at least, she amended.

Joss waved a casual hand towards the castle.
'Would that suit Madame?'

Lucy's eyes glistened. 'Do you mean it?'

He laughed. 'Sure do, ma'am. Once upon a time
it was the residence of the governor. It's a *pousada*
these days, but the conversion to modern comfort
is excellent, I promise. I've been here before.'

With Caroline? Lucy's reaction was overt
enough for Joss to interpret with ease, and he
flicked her cheek with a gentle finger.

'Caroline and I never got as far as a holiday

together, and even if we had, somewhere like St Tropez was more her style.' He grinned at her guilty expression. 'You have a very expressive face, Lucy.'

'Not exactly renowned for its beauty, you mean,' she said, resigned.

Joss looked blank. 'What are you talking about? Your face isn't just pretty, Lucy; it's intelligent, vivid, and it changes constantly, like a barometer, showing your moods. I never tire of looking at it.'

Lucy was so astonished by this they were at the Pousada do Castelo before she realised it. To her delight, they were given a room in the castle tower, and were obliged to leave the main part of the building and walk round the ramparts to get to it. But this time there was a double bed occupying the major part of the room. It was a four-poster, large and carved and impossible to ignore. A smile tugged at Joss's mouth at Lucy's reaction, which she was unable to hide.

'Come on,' he said briskly. 'Before I let you have a bath, let's walk round the walls like real, died-in-the-wool tourists—unless you're too tired.'

Lucy's assurances to the contrary were so fervent that an unholy gleam lit her husband's eyes as they went up to the old look-out path that led round the top of the town walls. The view was arresting enough to dispel Lucy's qualms about the bed as she gazed down at the houses and churches of the crowded little town, at the roofs glowing in variants of red above the blazing white of the walls. The streets seemed to zigzag in between the facades of the buildings without a straight line in sight, yet the general effect was of everything exactly right in its own particular place.

'Oh, Joss—I love it here.' On impulse, Lucy reached up and kissed Joss's cheek, and he smiled down at her, his arms tightening round her waist.

'I'm glad. Now then, let's go back and toss for who gets first crack at the bathroom.'

The bed looked less intimidating to Lucy when they regained their tower room. Joss took out some of his notes while she unpacked, and decided the matter of who was first in the bathroom by settling down at the dressing-table to work for a while. Lucy rummaged among her things for a paperback novel to read in the bath, and when she finally rejoined him much later, dressed in a linen skirt and cotton sweater, Joss looked up with an abstracted smile and glanced at his watch.

'Feel better?'

'Much. Though I'm still a bit punch-drunk from the drive.'

'Why not have a rest on the bed for a few minutes while I have a shower? Plenty of time before dinner.' He got up and stretched, and Lucy hopped up on the wide bed as he suggested, propping the snowy pillows behind her.

Joss came over and smoothed her hair. 'Am I tiring you out with all this exploring, Lucy?'

She shook her head. 'Of course not. I'm loving it. Apart from a school trip to Switzerland once, I've never been anywhere, and I don't want to miss a thing, I promise you. I'll be lazy for a few minutes, then I'll be raring to go.'

Lucy did her best to get interested in her book again when she was alone, but her eyelids kept drooping, and eventually she gave up and let herself doze. When she woke, it was dark in the room, except for the glowing tip of Joss's cigar. He was sitting on a tall, carved chair near the window, and as she stirred he got up and switched on the lamps. Lucy sprang off the bed, running her hand through her hair.

'Joss! Why didn't you wake me up?'

He stubbed out his cigar. 'What for? There's no rush. There never is in Portugal. Besides, the night is young by local standards.'

Joss was right. They ate a simple meal of fish and salad and excellent white wine in one of the little cafés in the town, then went out into the main square, where the local brass band was playing. Lucy felt as if she were under a spell, utterly enchanted by the music and the old buildings and the starry night sky. The people of the town were friendly as she wandered with Joss among them to sample the wine in several of the little bars tucked here and there. At one stage, costumed dancers performed with spirit and energy, and Lucy watched, her cheeks flushed with sun and wine—and happiness, she realised. She relaxed against Joss as he held her with an arm close about her waist, and realised she was *very* happy, and, in her present state of harmony with the world, thought it only right to tell him so.

Joss looked down at her, his eyes hooded, his skin dark against his white shirt. 'Are you, Lucy?' He had to bend to speak in her ear as the music played, and she felt his breath warm against her skin. 'Are you finally reconciled to throwing in your lot with the enemy?'

'Yes, I am. Perhaps it took this lovely holiday to convince me completely. Away from Abbotsbridge and all its associations, I mean. But here, in a foreign country—on neutral territory, you might say—I don't feel enmity of any kind any more.' In unspoken agreement they had turned to begin the walk back to the Pousada do Castelo, and she stopped in the narrow, dark street to face him. 'I appreciate your forbearance, Joss. About the—the —sleeping arrangements.'

He linked his hands very loosely about her waist, his teeth showing startlingly white for a moment. 'But I promised, Lucy, remember? I said you could sleep in peace until, if ever, you changed your mind.'

They resumed their walk in silence, and Lucy thought hard. Had she changed her mind? If she were honest, the presence of that double bed was a sharp reminder that life was short and youth was fleeting and Jonas Woodbridge was a man most women would consider themselves fortunate to have for a husband.

Neither of them said a word as they negotiated the rampants to their tower eyrie, and when Joss opened the heavy door for her, ushering her into the shadowy room, Lucy was filled with sudden curiosity about the others who had slept there before them; not only tourists like themselves, but the others long ago, in the days when this had been the castle of the governor. Lucy went to the foot of the bed, wondering how many brides had spent their wedding night beneath its canopy. She wanted to tell Joss she was ready to be his wife at last, but the words were extraordinarily difficult to frame. How did one phrase it? Flippancy, perhaps? She frowned, rejecting the idea of a joke, and Joss eyed her quizzically as he went into the bathroom. Lucy could hear him brushing his teeth, the sound of the shower hissing as he gave her time to undress, as he did every night, and suddenly she relaxed as the solution came to her. She stood quietly in the same spot, waiting until Joss came out of the bathroom with a towel knotted round his hips. He paused as he saw her standing where he'd left her, still in her white linen skirt and yellow cotton sweater, her jacket slung loosely from her shoulders.

'What's the matter, Lucy? Aren't you even going to bother to undress tonight?'

'I thought you might like to do it for me.' Her eyes met his steadily. 'If—if you wouldn't mind.'

Joss stood very still for a moment, then he walked towards her very slowly, his eyes glittering. Lucy stood her ground, ignoring her quaking knees and the thudding in her chest.

'I wish,' he said conversationally, 'that you'd made your request *before* I went into the bathroom.'

Lucy blinked. 'Why?'

'It would have been rather pleasant to enjoy a warm shower for once. My nightly douche of cold water is no doubt very character-building, but a bit of a shock to the system for one of my advancing years.' His smile was brilliant as he removed her jacket, tossing it on a chair, and Lucy gave a breathless little laugh as he drew her towards him until her cheek rested against the smooth skin of his chest.

'Why the cold showers?' she murmured, knowing why, but wanting him to tell her just the same.

His arms tightened. 'Don't be a hypocrite, Lucy Woodbridge. You're not that naïve!'

She tipped her head back and smiled up into his face, her eyes alight with mischief. 'I didn't think you'd be affected in the slightest—honestly! I mean, we've never even been obliged to share a bed yet.'

Joss's kindling look sent blood rushing to her cheeks. 'Lucy, my self-control has been stretched to its utmost merely by sharing the same room with you. For God's sake, couldn't you tell I've been going off my head with wanting to touch you, kiss you, grab you and hold you so tight your ribs crack?'

'Really?' Lucy's laugh was a delighted little sound that banished the last remnant of constraint between them. 'Then perhaps you'd like to make up for it now?'

With a choked sound, Joss dragged her hard against him, his mouth hungry on hers. Lucy responded with rapture, reaching up on tiptoe to run her hands through his thick, damp hair.

'Oh, Lucy, Lucy,' he muttered against her parted lips, and ran one hand down her spine to press her close against him as he kissed her deeply, his tongue finding hers. She gasped, clutching his hair, as her ragged breathing mingled with his.

Suddenly Lucy regretted asking Joss to undress her. She wanted to tear off her own clothes, push her naked breasts against his chest, feel his hard, aroused body against her own. But already Joss was pulling off her sweater with unsteady fingers. As her skin met his, her breath left her chest in a great rush, and Joss held her cruelly tight, kissing her roughly as his fingers sought the fastening of her skirt. Impatiently, Lucy pushed him away and stepped out of the skirt as it slid to the ground, stripping off her satin briefs in unashamed haste, then she was swung up in Joss's arms and they were together in the great bed that had suddenly become the one place in the world where she longed to be. But even as her body tensed and trembled under the caresses of Joss's mouth and hands, one minuscule part of her brain flew back to another time when they had come together like this, and as though he read her mind Joss raised his head and looked down at her, tenderness blended with the overt desire in his eyes.

'Don't be afraid, Lucy. This time I won't hurt you, I promise.'

She shook her head from side to side, her hair a wild, tangled darkness against the pillow. 'I'm not afraid, Joss. Please . . . *please* . . .'

In their urgency, neither had paused to turn off lights, and Lucy could see the sudden dark tide of colour which flooded Joss's face in the second before he began kissing her with mounting frenzy. The days of self-restraint had affected him more than he had shown, and now he was released from the bonds of his own rigid control at last, his hunger unleashed with an intensity which bordered on the desperate. His seeking mouth travelled her face and neck and shoulders, sending Lucy's blood coursing madly through her veins, her entire body on fire with response as it arched against his, and she cried out as his fingers found the sensitive place that throbbed for him. He brought her to a peak of longing she could hardly endure, and at the sound of her choked, astonished response the last vestige of control Joss possessed vanished. With a hoarse sound deep in his throat he arrived with force in the precise place Lucy wanted him to be, and for a moment they were still, eye to eye, breast to breast, unmoving except for the inner sensuous throb of their joining. In wonder, Lucy stared up into the beautiful, masculine features that were carved by desire to the likeness of some pagan deity, the eyes blazing down at her in fierce possession.

Then the moment was gone and Lucy's mind had no room left for fancy. The reality was the turbulence and heat and rhythm of now, as they moved together in convulsive accord, her voice murmuring his name over and over as she dug her fingers into his shoulders, wanting the ultimate, elusive rapture so badly she tossed her head back and forth on the pillows like a wild thing, until suddenly her cries were silenced as she drowned in such a cataclysm of sensation, she was only dimly aware that Joss cried out and shuddered in the throes of his own release. They fell asleep instantly, just as they were, too tired to break apart, and woke eventually in the first light of dawn with cramped muscles and aching limbs.

For a moment Lucy felt overwhelmingly shy, then Joss smoothed her tangled curls away from her damp forehead, his eyes alight with such tenderness, she felt better at once.

'Good morning, Lucy.' He smiled and shifted her so that she lay more comfortably in his arms. 'You look like a little girl found with her fingers in the jam.'

Lucy chuckled. 'If you mean guilty because I—well, because I enjoyed it all so much, I suppose you're right.'

'Didn't you expect to?' Joss nuzzled his mouth against her neck.

'No.'

'No?'

Lucy wriggled as his lips moved behind her ear. 'I haven't had much practice, you know.'

'Oh, I do.'

She sat up, looking down at him suspiciously. 'How?'

Joss rolled over on his back, clasping his arms behind his head. 'It *is* possible to tell, Lucy.' He eyed her warily. 'To try to phrase it politely, were some of the things we did——'

'*You* did!'

'All right, *I* did, new to you?'

Lucy linked her hand round her knees and lowered her chin on them. 'Well, yes. But it wasn't so much what you did, but how violently I responded. I just wasn't prepared for that.'

'Neither was I,' said Joss with feeling.

She looked at him from the corner of her eye. 'It was very different from the first time.'

Joss's lids flew up. 'That *was* different, Lucy. Entirely. I was fighting myself all the way, for one thing——'

'You were fighting me, too!'

He nodded ruefully. 'You were no help at all. I couldn't resist you in the end, and then I hurt you quite badly, and you cried. God, how you cried!'

'I felt so guilty and—and just plain bad!' Lucy bit her lip. 'I felt like the original scarlet woman. I mean, there was Simon, and Caroline, yet we still couldn't stop doing what we did.'

'It was my fault,' said Joss harshly. 'I should never have——'

Lucy laid a finger on his lips. 'It was my fault, too.'

He shut his eyes. 'I couldn't stand it when you

cried, Lucy. I felt like a murderer. And to cap it all I knew the experience was a painful disappointment to you. I'd never lost control of myself like that before—it was humiliating. Then, afterwards, you looked at me so expectantly with those wet, dark eyes, as though there was something you were waiting for me to do. Something that would make everything better.'

I didn't want you to *do* anything, thought Lucy wryly. I was just waiting for you to say you loved me. If you *had,* nothing else would have mattered. I was a starry-eyed little idiot who thought Joss Woodbridge wouldn't have, couldn't have made love to me for any other reason. It was when I realised you weren't going to say anything that I started to cry. She flushed as she realised Joss's eyes were open and watching her intently.

'What were you thinking?' he asked very quietly.

Lucy gave him a lop-sided smile. 'I was wondering if I was all right. Last night, I mean.'

Joss cleared his throat. 'Yes. I think we could definitely say that. More that just "all right".' He smiled slowly. 'As an experience, it was out of this world, Lucy, believe me.'

The look in his eyes made her shy again. 'Tom thinks we're too old for this kind of thing,' she reminded him.

'Tom, I sincerely hope, has no idea what he's talking about.' Joss's eyes roved over her savouringly as the covers fell to her waist. 'Caroline was absolutely right, you know. You possess the most beautiful breasts I've ever seen, Lucy Woodbridge.'

Lucy went scarlet and pulled up the sheet. 'And of course you've seen thousands!' She gave him a severe look. 'Besides which, I consider it very bad form to bring other women into the conversation on your honeymoon, Joss Woodbridge.'

'I apologise. Humbly.' Joss reached out a hand and ran it delicately down her spine; then, before she realised his intention he reached up and pulled her flat, rolling over on top of her, and holding her face in his hands. 'Shall I tell you what I want right now?'

Lucy's eyes gleamed with anticipation. 'Coffee? Breakfast? A nice warm shower?'

To her intense disappointment, he nodded briskly and jumped out of bed, grinning. 'That's it—the nice warm shower I've been yearning for.' Joss stood with hands on hips, laughing down at her, unselfconscious of his splendid nudity. Lucy's eyes strayed over the hard, tanned body, and broad shoulders and slim hips, the long, flat muscles and powerful legs, and suddenly she heaved over on to her stomach, burying her face in her pillow, hot with embarrassment at the sight of his body's response to her scrutiny. Joss laughed uproariously and scooped her up, bearing her off to the bathroom, where he turned the shower on them both and held her against him as he soaped her all over, his hands lingering over every curve and hollow until Lucy leaned against him, her legs trembling, and she grasped at his hair as he bent to take a hard, rose-red nipple in his mouth. Her knees buckled and Joss wrapped her in a towel and carried her back to bed and made love to her all over again, this time with all the lingering, slow expertise that had been beyond his power the night before.

When Lucy woke the second time the sun was

high and the day well advanced, and the room was
empty. Joss was nowhere to be seen. She sat up in
bed, disconcerted, then brightened as she saw a
note taped to the mirror.

'At the risk of taking too much for granted,'
Joss wrote, 'I think we've done enough travelling
for a while, Lucy, so I've gone on a little recce
while you slept off the exertions of the night. I
won't be long, so stay in bed and ring for breakfast
whenever you like. J.'

She did as he said, and lay on the bed reading
after almost wolfing the coffee and rolls brought
her. Her cheeks grew warm as she thought of the
reason for her unusual enthusiasm for breakfast.
Lovemaking, it seemed, gave one an appetite. It
was no surprise to find that Joss was a skilled lover,
despite the disaster of their first encounter. The
revelation of the night had been her own response
to him. Lucy tried hard to concentrate on her novel,
but her thoughts kept wandering away, and she
wondered where Joss had gone. She was longing for
him to come back, she realised, and slid off the bed
to look at herself in the mirror. There were tell-tale
marks on her shoulders and breasts, and her mouth
looked redder and fuller than usual. Faint shadows
showed beneath her shining eyes, and she grinned,
and stuck her tongue out at her reflection.

'Pretty obvious what you've been up to,' she
informed it. 'You've been acquiring that famous
glow Perdy gets from time to time.'

'And it suits you,' said a voice from the
doorway. Lucy spun round, embarrassed, and Joss
closed the door and crossed the room in three
strides, tossing a great bunch of red carnations on
the bed so he could snatch her in his arms and kiss

her. The kiss went one and on, and Lucy's dressing-gown slid from her shoulders as Joss's impatient hands pushed it aside so he could caress her breasts, which hardened and rose to his touch.

'Dear God,' he muttered at last, burying his face in her hair. 'You make me feel eighteen years old again——' He stiffened, his hands biting into her shoulders, and he raised his head to look at her, appalled. 'Lord, I'm a tactless swine. Lucy, love, I'm sorry, sorry.'

Lucy put up a hand to touch his face. 'It's all right, Joss. Don't get uptight. We can't watch our tongues all the time.' She turned to pick up the flowers, sniffing ecstatically. 'M'm, lovely.' She gave him a wicked smile. 'Are these a thank-you for being a good girl—or the reverse, I suppose, depending on which way you look at it?'

'I saw them in the town and thought of you.' Joss kissed her again. 'I've had a bit of luck, actually. I only booked this room for one night, so I tried to persuade the manager to let us stay longer.'

Lucy looked at him expectantly. 'And?'

'He was very apologetic, but it's already taken.' Joss paused tantalisingly. 'However, his wife's uncle's sister-in-law, or whatever, owns a villa near the coast, not far from here. Small, private beach, surrounded by pine trees, fully furnished and ours—if we like—for a couple of weeks. *Do* you like?'

'Oh, I do, I do!' If Joss had put the idea to her only the day before, Lucy would have had doubts about the prospect of two weeks alone with him in a villa miles from anywhere. Now, she found, she had none. 'That sounds a heavenly idea—when can we see it?'

'Right away. Senhora Vargas will meet us there. I've paid our bill, so pack your things, and if we like it we can move in at once. If we don't, we'll move on somewhere else.' Joss helped Lucy pack the few things she had taken out of her holdall, and a few minutes later they were ready to leave.

Lucy paused, trailing a hand over the carved bedpost. She smiled up at Joss. 'Most people dream of castles in Spain, don't they? My husband found a castle in Portugal for me, and it was utterly perfect.'

His eyes darkened and he moved towards her, then halted, taking a deep breath. 'I'll thank you for the compliment later, Mrs Woodbridge.'

An hour later they were standing on the veranda of a one-storey house which was very different from the ones Lucy had seen in travel brochures. This house was old and cool and sparsely furnished. It had high ceilings and shuttered windows and faded pink walls with plaster peeling in places. Every room led on to the veranda via double louvred doors, and the furniture was of wicker, and dark, carved wood, with striped curtains and bedhangings that could well have been there for a century or two.

'Not your average holiday villa,' commented Joss. 'Do you really like it, Lucy?'

Her smile was blissful. 'It's perfect.' She leaned on the veranda rail, looking out over the garden at the palms and geraniums and clustering pines that enclosed the Casa Rosada in perfect seclusion. Beyond the pines, the Atlantic rolled its surf and spray on the small portion of the Costa Verde private to the villa, which was the holiday retreat of the Vargas family, who were wine-shippers in Oporto. Normally the house was not rented to strangers, but Senhora Vargas, after hearing that the English couple were on their honeymoon, graciously consented to let them stay there, since none of her family required it this early in the season.

'How lucky we are,' said Lucy as she explored happily, exclaiming over the *azulejos*, the blue and white tiles which decorated the walls of the kitchen and bathroom. 'It's a big house to have only one bathroom,' she commented.

Joss stood propped against the veranda rail, laughing as she rushed from room to room. 'Enough for us, Lucy. We can toss a coin—or share.'

Lucy stood in one of the doorways, her eyes dark and dreaming as she thought of their shower together in the dawn, then went into his outstretched arms with such ardour that their tour ended abruptly in the room chosen for their bedroom.

'It's afternoon and the sun's shining,' she said indistinctly as he dropped kisses on the places he was laying bare as he undressed her.

'I don't know what they call it in Portugal,' Joss said huskily, 'but in Spain this is known as the siesta.'

His idea of a siesta lasted so long, Lucy's stomach gave a very unromantic rumble at last, reminding her that she was ravenous. Joss laughed and kissed the place that protested, then hauled her out of bed.

'Let's see if someone down in the local metropolis can feed us.'

It was only a few kilometres to the small fishing village Senhora Vargas had mentioned. They found it had a market which sold fresh vegetables and bread every morning, along with the day's catch of fish, but at this time of day a mouthwatering scent rose from the barbecues of several small cafés, where sardines and mackerel were grilling over charcoal. Lucy and Joss were welcomed with the friendly courtesy they had found everywhere in Portugal, and very quickly they were consuming as much fish as they could eat, accompanied by crusty bread, goat's cheese and a bowl of crisp salad. Some of the local wine was produced to wash it down, and afterwards the company of the local inhabitants proved so convivial, it was late before Joss drove Lucy back to the Casa Rosada.

The following days quickly fell into a routine Lucy enjoyed to the full. Each morning Joss would drive down to the village for bread and vegetables to eat with the eggs Lucy cooked in every way she could think of to make each breakfast different. Then Joss would work for a couple of hours while Lucy read and sunbathed and caught up on some of the sleep she missed out on during the long, pine-scented nights spent in her husband's arms.

'Are you never tired?' she asked one night, when at last they lay quiet.

'Of you, no.' Joss ran his lips along her jaw. 'But this is our honeymoon, remember. It would be surprising if making love were *not* the principal occupation of our nights.'

'Not only the nights,' Lucy pointed out, and he laughed and hugged her close.

'Just say the word if you think I'm too demanding, little wife.'

In all honesty, Lucy couldn't say he was. Joss never even had to ask. All it took was a look, a touch, and they were both lost, each one as urgent as the other. 'I'm equally to blame. Which is pretty astonishing, looked at objectively, when you consider how I dragged my feet at first.'

'That was because I am who I am—Joss Woodbridge, enemy number one from your point of view.'

Lucy couldn't deny it. 'Not that I've ever had much enthusiasm for anyone else's bed, to be honest.' She felt him shake with laughter.

'So this ravishing enthusiasm you display for my —my bed, is more in the way of novelty than a compliment to my expertise, I take it?'

' "Expertise" sounds as though you'd gone on a course, or something,' she objected. 'Surely the whole thing is more a natural instinct—stop laughing!'

'If it is, Lucy,' he said unsteadily, 'you possess it in spades!'

'Is that a compliment?'

'If it's a compliment to know your husband can't keep his hands off you, then yes, it is.'

Lucy was silent for a moment, staring at the moonlight chequering the floor with squares of light. 'Were you ever the same with Caroline?'

This time Joss laughed so much that Lucy was offended.

'What's so funny?' she demanded.

'You were the one who objected to previous partners being brought into the conversation,' Joss reminded her, when he could speak.

'Does that mean you couldn't keep your hands off

Caroline either?'

Which seemed to silence Joss completely, and Lucy lay very still, wondering not only if she'd gone too far, but whether her words were the simple truth, after all. And suddenly she wanted very badly to hear him say that he had never, even in the beginning, felt for Caroline the same overwhelming urgency he displayed towards his new bride. Lucy tried to be patient, waiting for him to answer, her mind going back to that fateful summer. She could remember herself with Simon and Joss vividly, but when she tried to picture Joss with Caroline, all she could bring to mind was the girl's cool, blonde perfection, and the resentment Caroline had harboured for the fiancé who not only spent too much time in the study, but when he did emerge from it demonstrated an undisguised penchant for his brother's girlfriend.

Joss's voice, when he finally spoke, startled her as he sat up in bed and turned on the bedside lamp. 'I'm going to get myself a drink, Lucy. Would you like something?'

'Yes, please.' She looked at him uncertainly, trying to read his face. 'Orange juice, or whatever you can find.'

Joss pulled on his dressing-gown and went out, and Lucy searched for her nightgown, feeling a need for protective cover. She propped some pillows behind her, and was sitting bolt upright when Joss returned with the drinks.

He looked at her tense face and grinned. 'Don't look so worried. I'm not going to eat you.'

Lucy relaxed a little. She thanked him for the fruit juice and sipped it as he settled himself beside her.

'Lucy,' he began, 'perhaps this is as good a time as any for clearing up whatever misconceptions we still harbour about each other.'

Her fingers gripped the glass convulsively. 'What do you mean, Joss?'

'On the subject of Caroline, for one.'

'Joss, please, you don't have to say anything. I'm sorry I ever mentioned her.' All at once, Lucy didn't want to hear what he had to say.

'I think you should know one or two things, just the same.' Joss's tone was the calm impersonal one he used for dictating. 'I drifted into an engagement to Caroline not just because she was so beautiful, but because she made the running. She was older than me by a couple of years, and in spite of her looks had never managed to catch anyone with enough money to make him eligible to her as a husband.'

'I see,' said Lucy quietly.

'One night there was a full moon when I was taking her home after some party, and before I knew it I heard myself asking her to marry me, though it was very inconvenient at the time as I was trying to work to a deadline for my first book, which was about Australian aborigines, if you remember.'

'Oh, yes, I remember.'

Joss stroked her hand, then went on. 'What I am trying to say is that I was never really in love with Caroline, nor even as taken with her physical charms as she would have wished, which made her furious. Her vanity couldn't take it.'

Lucy's hand tightened on his in sympathy. 'I never had the least idea. I knew Simon wasn't awfully fond of her, of course.'

'So did I!'

'But he never told me about the rest of it.'

'I made him promise not to. Particularly when one night she flew into a screaming rage in front of Simon, and kindly informed me that my sole attraction was my money.' Joss shook his head. 'Caroline, when in full spate, could muster an amazing vocabulary of invective, and screamed things at me no man would care to repeat, let alone have his younger brother hear.'

'Simon never said a word.' Lucy felt stunned. She had always been totally sure Simon shared everything with her. 'Is that why you began to drink more heavily?'

'No. I had other reasons for hitting the bottle. Reasons Caroline suspected and bitterly resented.'

Lucy looked up at him questioningly, but he looked lost in thought.

'Her real sin, from my point of view,' Joss said at last, 'was in transferring her attentions from me to Simon.'

'*What?* You're not serious!'

'I am. Caroline is the type of woman who can't survive without constant reassurance about her charms, even though she wasn't really hot-blooded at all—just stupendously vain.'

'Simon never said anything. I knew he didn't like Caroline much——'

'*Like* her! He was terrified of her. She did her best to seduce the poor kid. But of course, since he had you, she didn't stand much chance, did she? I was so relieved when Manual Vargas came on the scene, I would have settled a dowry on Caroline to have him take her off my hands.'

Lucy felt all at sea. 'I thought you were so cut up

about it you couldn't stand being sober.'

'That's what I intended you—and everyone else
—to think.' Joss slid an arm round Lucy's waist
and held her close. 'I used to watch you running
around the place with Simon that summer, and
envy him so bitterly I began to drink.'

Lucy lay very still. 'You envied him, Joss?'

He gave an odd, strained laugh. 'Simon seemed
to have everything I wanted at that particular time.
Youth, freedom, that incredibly sunny disposition
of his—and you.'

She swallowed hard. 'I knew you were fond of
me, of course——'

'*Fond!* I wanted you violently, Lucy. That
summer you were so brown and glowing, your hair
was longer then, a great untidy mass hanging down
your back, and you always seemed to be in shorts,
and tennis shirts that were too tight.'

'My school sports kit, shrunk from my own
amateur laundering.' Lucy smiled wryly. 'I hated
looking so childish—longed for beautiful clothes
like Caroline, so you would notice me.'

Joss turned her in his arms and kissed her hard.
'Notice you!' he muttered against her mouth. 'I
couldn't keep my eyes off you. When you played
tennis with Simon the things clung to you like a
second skin. Caroline knew damn well how it was
with me, too. Made out I was some kind of pervert,
too busy lusting after a schoolgirl to pay attention
to a grown woman.'

Lucy rubbed her cheek against his. 'Were you,
Joss?'

'I thought I'd proved it rather conclusively one
unforgettable afternoon that summer.' He looked
down into her eyes, and Lucy flushed and her lids

dropped to hide them.

'That was an accident—circumstances beyond our control. But the thing I couldn't understand, Joss, is why you were so cruel to me when I told you I was pregnant? You didn't seem in the least fond of me that day!'

His arms tightened mercilessly. 'Shock, anger, jealousy—take your pick. I was pole-axed at the mere thought of your letting Simon make love to you. Somehow it had never occurred to me that you and Simon had that sort of relationship. To me, you'd always been a happy-go-lucky pair of children together, but God knows, it was natural enough for you to turn to him after the débâcle of the experience with me. His lovemaking must have been a welcome contrast, and a damn sight more preferable than mine.' A shudder went through him, and Lucy hugged him fiercely.

'Don't, Joss—stop thinking about the past,' she said passionately.

He put a finger under her chin and turned her face up to his. 'Have you finally forgiven me, Lucy?'

Her dark eyes were luminous as they met his. 'Joss, let's never think about any of it again. We're together now, no Simon, no Caroline, just you and me. And Caroline must have been out of her stupid mind if she really preferred your money to you, which I don't believe for a moment. Nor,' she added, with a cat-like little smile, 'do I believe that lots of women haven't reassured you on that particular point over the past ten years!'

Joss smiled, to her relief, and cupped her face in his hands. 'True enough, but no woman has ever made me feel the way you do, Lucy.'

The deep sincerity in Joss's voice gave Lucy inspiration. She sprang out of bed and very slowly peeled off her nightgown, then tossed it on the floor and stalked round the bed. Joss looked startled for an instant, then lay very still, his possessive eyes moving over her body like a caress. She stood for a moment, proud and erect, watching as he began to breathe more heavily, then with deliberation she revolved, clasping her hands behind her head until she'd turned full circle. Joss's eyes glittered in his taut face, and she smiled.

'I'm not seventeen any more,' she said huskily, 'but I don't think I've deteriorated too badly. Do you still fancy me, Joss?'

His response was to haul her into bed, his mouth too occupied with kissing her to answer. As his lips began to move all over her body, Lucy gloried in the unashamed need of his onslaught, her hands sliding over his back, her fingers soothing at first, then digging into his muscles as his clever hands made her gasp. She thrust herself against him and said 'Now!' through clenched teeth, but Joss laughed exultantly, in full command by this time, and continued the exquisite torture until Lucy thought she would die if he didn't take her. At last she found the way to persuade him, her fingers closing on him in a caressing grasp that brought a ragged groan from him and for a moment he was vanquished. Then a glorious smile of victory lit his eyes as their bodies slotted together like two halves of a whole, and Lucy's smile reflected his for an instant before she was lost in the heat and magic of their lovemaking.

When Lucy woke she was still held close in Joss's

arms, and her eyes opened to meet his with such an unguarded look of joy that Joss closed his own for an instant before rubbing his cheek against hers.

'I love you, Lucy,' he said, and she lay very still, sure she was dreaming. Joss raised his head, smiling at her with a tenderness that took her breath away. 'Do you mind?'

Lucy was utterly overwhelmed. 'I—I thought you just wanted Tom.'

'I *do*. I'm very fond of Tom. But I find I love his mother far more than I had ever expected to love any woman, just to remove any doubts you might have on the subject.' Joss's jewel-bright eyes held hers. 'Dare I ask how you feel about *me*?'

Lucy had no ready answer. After keeping Jonas Woodbridge out of her life for so long, her feelings for him had undergone such a sea-change during the last few weeks, she hardly knew how she felt about him. She knew quite well she no longer resented him. And to enjoy what they did together in this very bed, Lucy felt certain she must be at least *in* love with him. God knows, he must be the handsomest man I've ever known, she thought. And he'd kind and thoughtful and generous—and he's the husband I promised to love, honour and cherish in church in front of half of Abbotsbridge.

'I don't know much about love between a man and a woman,' she said honestly. 'I know I'm happy with you, Joss. You make me feel cherished and special. Apart from which, I seem to go up in flames the moment I touch you, as must be only too obvious, so I suppose I must love you.'

His eyes gleamed with wry amusement. 'Don't go into too many raptures, Lucy. I might get above myself.'

She smiled. 'I'm not given very much to superlatives.' She eyed him anxiously. 'Have I hurt you, Joss?'

He kissed her gently. 'No, Lucy.' But a little of the light in his eyes had dimmed, she saw with a pang.

'Perhaps if I persevere, you may reciprocate in full one day,' he said lightly, and detached himself from her arms. 'In the meantime, I shall go to the village for bread and onions and peppers, and you shall console me with one of your Spanish omelettes—or even a Portuguese one, if you know how to concoct such a thing.'

CHAPTER EIGHT

IT WAS less easy than Lucy expected to settle down to life once the honeymoon was over. Her zest for treasure-hunting at local sales had diminished, and even the discovery of a genuine Thonet bentwood table one day failed to rouse her enthusiasm as it would have done only weeks earlier.

'You look tired,' commented Joss towards the end of Lucy's first week back at the shop.

'I am.' Lucy yawned. 'Yet these days I'm utterly spoiled. I never do a thing once I'm home.'

Joss's eyes lit at the word 'home', but his smile was teasing as he joined her on the big leather chesterfield. 'Mrs Benson has always spoiled you, Lucy, admit it.'

'Oh, I do.' She leaned back against his encircling arm, wriggling closer as it tightened about her waist. 'How's the book going?'

'Another week and it should be finished. I'm a bit behind, I'm afraid.'

'I suppose getting married in the middle of it didn't help.'

'I intended working more in Portugal,' he reminded her, and tipped her face up to his. 'You proved very distracting, you witch.'

'Sorry! I didn't try to be.'

'You didn't have to!' Joss kissed her lingeringly. 'As has been proved beyond all question, I am putty in your hands.'

Lucy climbed on his lap, twining her arms round his neck. 'Have I ever told you,' she said between kisses, 'how much I approve of the arrangement?'

At which point Mrs Benson came in to say dinner was ready and Lucy scrambled off her husband's knee in ungraceful haste, while Joss roared with laughter at her embarrassment.

'We *are* married,' he said, as they sat down at the table.

'I know, I know. But we needn't shock people.' Lucy smiled at him. 'And we'll have a chaperon this weekend. It's Tom's *exeat*.'

'Can you get Perdy to fill in, or shall I collect him on my own tomorrow?'

'Perdy's off to give one of her talks this Saturday at a craft exhibition up north, so I'll have to hold the fort myself.' Lucy gave him a glowing look. 'Tom would rather you fetched him. He'll be thrilled.'

'I'm only too pleased. And *this* time Mrs Benson can pass the dreaded trunk to Edna from Bridge Farm when she comes to help with the laundry.'

Lucy had no objection to that at all. It was one chore she was heartily glad to surrender. Her lack of energy irritated her, and to her utter dismay later that night, for once Lucy felt too tired to respond when Joss began to caress her after they were in bed.

'I'm sorry,' she said, mortified. 'I don't know why—it's not because I don't *want* to—at least not in my mind. But the rest of me feels like a rag doll.'

Joss held her close, one hand stroking her hair. 'It's not surprising, sweetheart. We've been married several weeks now, and for most of that time we've made love more than I'd have believed possible. I'm quite proud of myself, to be honest.'

Lucy chuckled. 'You, as you know perfectly well, Joss Woodbridge, are the most superlative lover. I'm a very fortunate lady.'

'Thank you, darling. And I'm a very fortunate man.' He kissed her tenderly. 'Now go to sleep.'

The sale of Holly Lodge was going through smoothly, Tom was coming home for the weekend, and she was married to the most exciting, gorgeous man in the whole wide world, Lucy decided, as she closed the shop that particular Friday evening. It was rather worrying to find she had nothing to worry about. Laughing at herself, Lucy drove home to bathe and array herself in a new dress, ready to greet her son and husband when they arrived. After a flurry of excited greetings, Tom was ravenous for the meal Mrs Benson served without a trace of apology. No one would have suspected that canned tomato soup, followed by sausages, baked beans, chips and coleslaw weren't a regular choice for dinner at Abbot's Wood.

'Gosh,' said Tom, tucking in with rapture. 'Mrs Benson's a super cook!'

Joss conveyed his sentiments to the lady in question when she arrived with apple pie, chocolate ice cream, canned peaches and a selection of cheeses, in a masterly effort to suit everyone's taste. Mrs Benson smiled, gratified, as she cleared away the main course.

'Nice to see a lad eat well when he's growing.'

Normally this was the type of remark calculated to make Tom cringe, but Mrs Benson, it seemed, could do no wrong as far as he was concerned. Still talking nineteen to the dozen, he ate a portion of everything, a second one of ice cream and peaches, then asked if he could be excused, because Benson had promised to show him his collection of fishing flies.

'I didn't even know Benson *had* a collection of fishing flies,' said Joss, laughing.

Lucy shook her head admonishingly. 'How very remiss of you. And how silly of me to imagine our holiday in Portugal could have any interest whatsoever compared with the excitement of T Drummond's thirty not out at the first housematch of the cricket season!'

They laughed together and went back to the study to watch a programme about an archaeological excavation in Turkey while they waited for Tom to tear himself away from the delights of the Bensons' company.

'I suppose you'll be thinking about Brazil soon,' said Lucy wistfully when the programme finished.

'I'm afraid so.' Joss kissed her drooping mouth. 'I wish I could take you with me, Lucy, but I don't think you'd enjoy this particular trip. The climate in the Amazon Basin can be pretty gruelling.'

'I couldn't come anyway. There's the shop, and Tom.'

Joss hesitated a he looked at her despondent face. 'Lucy,' he said, after a while, 'I don't want to butt in on your own private territory, but do you really need to keep on the shop now there's no financial necessity? Or if you don't want to give it up, perhaps you could get in someone to help fulltime, leave you free just to do the buying, or whatever.'

Lucy looked at him thoughtfully. Joss, unknown to himself, was only putting into words something she'd been mulling over in her mind ever since their return to Portugal. 'I'll give it some thought,' she said eventually. 'The shop has been part of my life so long, I wouldn't know what to do with myself, perhaps, if I did give it up.'

Joss made no further effort to persuade her, and since Tom came bursting in at that juncture the subject was dropped. In the excitement of the arrangements for the proposed fishing trip next day, Lucy took a back seat while her son eagerly discussed the best stretches of river to try with Joss. I could, she thought wryly, be forgiven for feeling a little left out of things one way and another, now Tom has enlarged his horizons to include Joss and the Bensons.

'Perhaps you'd like to ask young Ben Todd along too,' she suggested.

Tom thought it over carefully, winding a strand of hair round a grubby finger. 'Not *this* time,' he said finally. 'I'd prefer to go with Joss on my own first.'

From the slight gruffness in his voice when he asked what Tom would like to drink, it was plain Joss was deeply touched by the boy's answer.

The fishermen were still out, to Lucy's surprise, when she got home the following evening.

'They're late, Mrs B,' she said, as she went into the kitchen. 'No phone message, I suppose?'

'No, Miss Lucy.' Mrs Benson gave a worried glance at the clock. 'But it's only half-past five. Don't fret. No doubt the fish are biting and they've lost track of the time. You go off and have your bath, and I expect they'll be here by the time you're dressed.'

Lucy had finished her bath, dressed, and worked

herself into a high old state of nerves by the time the Land Rover finally arrived. Limp with relief, she ran to the top of the stairs to find Benson helping Joss with Tom, who was smiling valiantly, but a bit green around the gills as Joss gave him a piggy-back up to his room.

'Nothing to worry about,' Joss assured Lucy, panting.

'I fell down a bank and cut my foot on a broken bottle,' said Tom in disgust, as he clung to Joss's shoulders.

Lucy was her father's daughter, trained from babyhood not to fuss over minor accidents. 'Right, then,' she said briskly, as Joss deposited Tom on the bed in his new room. 'Let's have a look.'

'I was pulling off his wader,' said Joss, kneeling to remove Tom's sock, 'and he shot out of it suddenly, like toothpaste from a tube. He careered down a slope before I could stop him. A good thing you'd provided me with some plasters.'

'When you know Tom better, you'll learn it's best never to set foot outside the door without them,' said Lucy. 'It's not so long since he had a bad fall in the quad in school and cut his head open.'

'I told Joss that,' said Tom with pride, trying not to wince as his mother removed a large square of plaster from the sole of his foot. 'They were even going to give me some blood, but I didn't need it in the end.'

'Most impressive,' agreed Joss.

'Did you catch any fish, by the way?' asked Lucy.

'Three!' Tom grinned widely. 'But we threw them back.'

'They weren't a bad size,' said Joss, and grinned back. 'Right then, old chap. Can you negotiate the stairs to come down to dinner, or would you prefer a tray in bed in front of your television?'

'Could I?' Tom looked at his mother for confirmation. 'Would it be a lot of trouble?'

'I'm sure Benson will be only too delighted to oblige,' said Joss drily. 'And that cut will heal faster if you stay off your foot for a while.' He turned to Lucy. 'I'll have a shower while you do the Florence Nightingale bit.'

Over dinner, Joss kept up a flow of witty conversation once he'd gone over the details of the accident. Lucy looked at him thoughtfully as he told her about an amusing literary lunch he'd attended once, discussed the programme they'd watched the night before, various items in the daily paper. Something was wrong, she thought with foreboding. It was like being at a dinner party, next to someone obliged to keep up a barrage of small talk. She responded as animatedly as someone could who felt as if the sword of Damocles hung over her head throughout the entire meal.

Had she offended him in some way? She hadn't kissed him in greeting, to be sure, but since Joss had been hefting her son up the stairs at the time he was hardly likely to consider it a grave oversight. Or perhaps he was more put out by her lack of response recently than he'd let on. Whatever the cause of Joss's witty, brittle manner, Lucy was heartily glad when dinner was over, Tom had been paid a final visit, and she and Joss were in the study at last, free from interruption.

'What's wrong, Joss?' she asked, unable to bear it a moment longer. 'Is it something I've done?'

Joss took his time over lighting a cigar. 'No,
Lucy. It's more in the nature of something you
haven't done.'

'I know I didn't give you much of a welcome,'
she put in quickly, 'but in all the fuss over
Tom——'

'Credit me with more maturity than that!'

Lucy's heart contracted at the scathing note in
his voice. These days, she was used to the heady
security of Joss's approbation. Without it, she felt
cold. 'Will you explain?' she asked steadily.

'I found Tom's story about his fall in school
extremely interesting.'

Lucy looked at him blankly. 'Really?'

Joss's nostrils flared slightly as he eyed her
closely. 'He was rather proud of his blood group.
A bit out of the ordinary, isn't it?'

'So I believe. Quite unlike mine.' Her heart
began to pound.

Joss's eyebrows rose. 'What *is* yours, Lucy?'

'Very ordinary—Group O Positive.'

'So was Simon, oddly enough, whereas
mine——' Joss paused, his eyes holding hers.
'Mine is A Negative, like Tom's.'

Lucy stared at him dumbly.

'Nothing to say, Lucy?' he prompted. 'No?
Then I'll go on. My father had the same blood
group as Tom and me, too. He had several
transfusions during his last illness, which is how I
happen to know. Simon must have inherited *his*
blood group from his natural father, which is why
it's different.'

'His natural father!' echoed Lucy, thunderstruck. 'What do you mean?'

Joss settled back in his chair, his face remote

and withdrawn. 'I shall elucidate. Simon was the son of my aunt, Olivia Woodbridge, my father's sister. The secret was the family skeleton in the closet. I had no idea of it myself until my father fell ill at the last and decided to tell me. Simon never learned the truth.' He gave her a faint, disquieting smile. 'As you know better than most, Lucy, these accidents happen. To my aunt, almost thirty years ago, it was a deep disgrace, particularly since the man in question was already married. At this juncture, my mother stepped in. Her health had been deteriorating from some time, and she persuaded my father to let her come to Olivia's rescue by giving out that pregnancy was the cause of her own indisposition. My aunt went away for a period, and eventually the fruit of her shame—I believe that was the popular phrase—was smuggled back to Abbot's Wood and looked on as the new Woodbridge child. Since my mother died not long afterwards, it was assumed Simon's birth had been the cause. No one thought it odd that Aunt Olivia took up residence again to look after us all, or knew that she devoted the rest of her life to bringing up her son to look on her as his aunt instead of his mother.'

The silence in the room lay between them like a tangible barrier as Lucy's eyes, dark with guilt, met the cold blue gaze of her husband.

'Well?' he asked caustically. 'Cat got your tongue, Lucy?'

Lucy looked away. It was strange. Now that the long-dreaded moment was finally here she was almost relieved. But frightened, too. Frightened Joss would turn against her as he had once before. There was an implacable look about the set of his jaw that warned her not to expect too much in the way of sympathy. Lucy braced herself. It was useless to try to bluff it out, to insist that the blood group was a coincidence.

Her expressive face told Joss something of what she was thinking, as usual. 'Are you going to deny Tom's mine, Lucy?'

'No.'

'Very sensible, since you and Simon are unlikely to have produced a child with a blood group like Tom's—and mine. I'm not sure it would stand up in a court of law in a paternity suit, since it's more likely a blood group proves who is not the father than who is. Nevertheless, I assume I am Tom's father.' His eyes were challenging. 'Unless you managed to sandwich in a third lover that summer, of course—one with the requisite blood type.'

Lucy swallowed her fierce resentment. Joss was entitled to his anger, she conceded. 'No, I did not.' she said at last. 'I suppose it was foolish to think I could keep it a secret for ever, but I'm not well up on blood groups, and of course I knew nothing about your Aunt Olivia.' Her eyes shadowed. 'Poor lady. How sad it must have been for her, always pretending to be Simon's aunt . . .'

'Your sentiments do you credit,' Joss interposed coldly, 'but at this moment, fond though I was of my aunt, my interest is centred on you. And Tom.' For a moment, it seemed he would jump up and yank her out of her chair, but with an effort that made Lucy quake inwardly Joss sat deadly still, his eyes burning into hers. 'Why in God's name did you never tell me?' he bit out after a while. 'That last day when Simon came rushing into the study and announced you were having his baby and he wanted to marry you at once I turned on him, in sheer jealous rage, and forbade it. He looked at me as though he'd never seen me before, then rushed out again . . .' He broke off, looking sick.

'I know,' said Lucy quietly. 'He came back to Holly Lodge and told me you were furious, and to make matters worse he'd bumped into Edna, who was a housemaid here then, and realised she'd heard the whole thing. Poor Simon, he was in a complete spin, but kept telling me not to worry, that he'd marry me and say the baby was his, whoever the father was.'

Joss stared at her incredulously. '*Whoever* the father was?'

Lucy's eyes dropped, and she nodded miserably. 'I didn't tell him it was you. I just couldn't bring myself to disillusion him about his wonderful brother.'

'Why the devil didn't he think the child was his?'

'Because Simon and I were never lovers,' said Lucy flatly.

Joss jumped to his feet and stood over her, breathing hard. 'You mean to say Tom owes his existence to that one time we——' He sat down again abruptly and stared into the fire with brooding eyes.

Lucy gazed at his profile, knowing only too well the picture he could see in his mind's eye: a particularly hot, humid afternoon, no different from a dozen others that summer when she had played tennis with Simon on the old grass court at the back of the house. But that day Simon had stolen off afterwards to one of his illicit flying lessons, and she had taken advantage of his offer of a shower before she cycled home. Lucy's nails bit

into the palms of her hands at the memory. She
had thought no one was in the house, but Joss had
been locked in his study, working, until the heat
drove him to take a shower to clear his head. Lucy
hadn't even bothered to lock the bathroom door,
and it was difficult to know who suffered the
greater shock when Joss, with only a towel
wrapped around his hips, found Lucy Drummond
in the last place he expected her to be.

Frozen in tableau, they had stared at each other
in astonishment for a split second before Lucy
dived for a towel at the precise moment Joss
snatched at it to hand over to her. If they had never
touched, thought Lucy despairingly, nothing might
have happened. But that one touch had been
enough, too much, for both of them. With a
tortured groan, Joss pulled her against him as he
kicked the door shut behind him, his mouth
finding her blindly with a hunger she responded to
so wholeheartedly he was lost, and they sank to
their knees together, battered down by the feelings
surging over them. Even then Joss had tried to tear
himself away, but Lucy, all her wildest dreams
come true, had clung to him fiercely, and in her
innocence deprived him of the last of his self-
control. Their coming together had been sudden
and violent and utterly inevitable. Lucy had gasped
with pain, and all too soon it was over and they
were staring at each other, wild-eyed, aghast at
what had happened, both of them racked with guilt
and regret. And Lucy had wept bitter tears that
convinced Joss he could never hope to redeem
himself in her eyes again.

'I couldn't face you afterwards,' said Joss, not
looking at her. 'I assumed I'd disgusted you.'

'And I thought I'd disgusted *you*.' Lucy sighed heavily. 'So I tried to keep out of your way. Simon knew something was wrong, he kept on plaguing me to tell him. So when I found out I was pregnant I was so horrified I *did* tell him, but not—not about you. He didn't even press me for details, he just went dashing off to you and Edna did the rest. My guilty secret was public property in Abbotsbridge from the first, except that Edna got the wrong father for my child.' She drew in a long, shaking breath. 'Simon was so upset that day that I went with him to the aerodrome for once because it was his solo flight and I felt he should have company for his big occasion. It was *my* fault Simon got killed. His mind wasn't on what he was doing.'

Joss looked up sharply, shaking his head. 'No, Lucy. If it was anyone's fault, it was mine for raging at him like a maniac.'

'Perhaps it was just fate,' said Lucy sadly.

'Perhaps.' Joss looked at her questioningly. 'And the day you came to see me, after Simon was killed; were you going to tell me the truth, Lucy?'

His eyes hardened. 'Yes, I was. Unfortunately, you just didn't want to know.'

Their second fateful encounter had been even less happy than the first. For days Lucy had tried to pluck up enough courage to visit Joss, but every time she set out for Abbot's Wood her courage had ebbed away before she reached the gates, and she'd cycled back home again, utterly miserable and desperate. Then she'd heard Jonas Woodbridge was setting out on his travels again and she'd had no alternative. If she wanted to talk to Joss, she would have to do it at once.

Mrs Benson had directed Lucy to the summerhouse, where Joss, she said, had taken to spending most of his time since Simon's death. Lucy trudged through the garden, past the old grass court and on to the summerhouse overlooking the river which formed the boundary of Woodbridge land. Joss had been sprawled in an old deck-chair, just staring, a book hanging from the lax fingers of one hand. Lucy's courage failed her at the sight of him, and she would have run away as fast as her long brown legs could carry her, but a twig cracked beneath her sandal and Joss spun round. He sprang to his feet, and she quailed before the blazing hostility in his eyes, the blue eyes that were so like Simon's.

'Well?' he asked coldly. 'What can I do for you, Lucy Drummond?'

'I heard you were going away,' she said faintly.

'And you came to wish me bon voyage? How thoughtful.'

'That's not why I'm here, Joss.' How on earth was she to put it into words, she thought miserably. 'I—I have a problem.'

'*You* have a problem.' He laughed shortly. 'Don't we all! But do go on. If your problem is guilt over Simon, then it is, at least, one we both share.'

Lucy struggled to find words to tell him they shared more than that, but the task was so impossible, sweat broke out in the palms of her hands and dampened the hair at her temples. This man was a cold stranger, nothing at all to do with the passionate lover who had been as helpless as she in the grip of their mutual passion.

'I'm pregnant, Joss,' she said baldly at last.

'I know that,' he said, glaring at her. 'Simon told me that last day.' He was breathing hard, a vein throbbing at his temple. 'And now I suppose you've come to lay the blame at Simon's door. Not so fast, young woman. Simon's dead. He can't defend himself. But *I* can. What proof can you give me that Simon is the father? Well? Tell me!' And he shook her.

At his words, something died inside young Lucy Drummond, and a fierce pride took root in its place. Her chin lifted and she looked Jonas Woodbridge in the eye.

'Take your hands off me, please,' she said with quiet dignity, and Joss had the grace to look discomfited as he moved back. 'I have no proof, of course. It never occurred to me I'd need any.'

'But it occurred to you that financial support was necessary, I suppose. Woodbridge money, to be precise.'

'Not even that.' Lucy felt she'd aged a hundred years since her arrival. 'I think I came in search of comfort, sympathy. I don't know. Whatever it was, I came to the wrong shop. Goodbye, Joss. I shan't ever bother you again.'

'Lucy, wait——'

Lucy turned and ran. She raced for her bicycle as though the hounds of hell were at her heels, frantic to get away from Abbot's Wood.

She came back to the present with a jolt, and shivered a little as she looked at Joss. 'I intended to tell you, but your reaction to Simon as the father of my child was violent enough. It was utterly impossible then to say *you* were the one who made me pregnant. You'd really have thought I was cashing in, wouldn't you? Not poor dead Simon, but rich live Jonas. So I peddled like fury all the way to Abbotsbridge and told Cassie Page instead. But not a word as to who the father was, then or ever, only the terrifying fact that I was pregnant. The conclusions everyone drew about the paternity of my baby were due to Edna Baker, not me.'

Joss rubbed a hand over his haggard face. 'But why in God's name didn't you tell me afterwards, Lucy? It wasn't long before I came to my senses and tore round to your place to beg you to marry me, to say I was willing to be a father to Simon's child—anything, just so I could have you.'

Lucy went deadly white. 'Is *that* why you came? I thought your idea was to offer me money.'

He flinched. 'Which is why your door stayed shut in my face.'

'I persuaded myself I hated you.'

'With reason. Not,' he added harshly, 'more than I did myself. The look of horror on your face haunted me. I felt like a murderer.' He jumped to his feet. 'It's so incredible! Part of me wants to go down on my knees and thank God for my son, yet at the same time I can't help thinking of all the time we've wasted.

Lucy eyed him dispassionately. 'Is that what annoys you, then, Joss? That I deprived you of ten years of Tom's company?'

He returned the look with interest. 'That, too. But you sentenced us all, Lucy. By keeping my part in Tom's birth to yourself, you not only denied him a father, but yourself a husband and me a wife.'

'And how was I to know how you really felt?' she demanded. 'To me you were my knight in shining armour, a paragon of perfection I looked up to in awe. The things you said absolutely flayed me alive.'

There was silence between them, while Lucy twisted the ring on her finger, looking pensive. After a while she looked up at him with a strange, sad little smile. 'But we got married in the end, Joss, after all. If this were a fairy-tale, wouldn't that be happy ever after?'

He bent to pull her to her feet, and held her by the shoulders. 'We could have been happy so much sooner, Lucy.'

Her eyes met his without wavering. 'We can't put back the clock. All we have is now, and whatever future fate has in store for us. Are you very angry with me, Joss?'

His mouth twisted. 'I have no right to be, but I can't get those ten years out of my mind.'

'They were no picnic for Tom and me, either!'

His grasp tightened cruelly. 'I'm well aware of that, Lucy. But the choice was yours.'

'That isn't fair! I never in my wildest dreams imagined you'd want . . .' She trailed into silence before the smouldering look in Joss's eyes.

'Want Tom?' he asked silkily. 'Or you?'

'If I ever imagined you'd want anything, I certainly thought it was more likely to be Tom than his unmarried mother!' Lucy saw him wince, and felt fierce satisfaction, suddenly wanting to hurt, wanting him to know a little of the pain he had once inflicted on her. Their eyes locked, and Joss breathed deeply, then let her go.

'So what do we do now?' he asked quietly.

Do? Lucy looked at him in alarm. 'What do you mean?'

He shrugged. 'Do you still want to stay married to me, Lucy?'

Her blood ran cold. 'Not if you don't, Joss.' Her voice sounded odd. Not like hers at all, she thought, and watched Joss's hands clench and a tell-tale vein throb at the corner of his mouth. She longed to know what was going on in his mind, but his lids shuttered his eyes, and his face could have been carved from wood for all the clue it gave to his feelings.

'It would be rather shattering for Tom, don't you think, if we separated now?' said Joss without looking at her, and Lucy sat down abruptly, aghast to find that for a moment she'd forgotten Tom.

'Yes. It would.' She hesitated. 'Would—would you like me to tell Tom? That you're his father, I mean?'

Joss shook his head. 'I have no right to expect it. And frankly I feel apprehensive at the prospect. He'll probably want to know why the hell I left you to struggle alone all these years. I can't quite see how to explain to a boy of his age that a man can be an utter lunatic about some things.'

Lucy rubbed wearily at her eyes. 'I could say it was my fault,' she offered.

Joss looked bleak. 'My behaviour may not always have been exemplary, Lucy, but I think we can safely say I have no intention of letting you shoulder the blame for our particular situation.'

'Then let's leave it for now.' Depression enveloped Lucy like fog. Whoever said confession was good for the soul had it all wrong. 'The opportunity will probably occur naturally some time. If—if we go on as though nothing had happened. Is that what you want?'

'I want a great deal more than that, Lucy, but it will do for now.'

She coloured at the look in his eyes and got up to go. 'I'm tired, Joss. I think I'll go to bed.'

There was a nasty little silence.

'Perhaps I should sleep in the dressing-room tonght,' said Joss without inflection.

Lucy felt stricken. 'Whatever you think best.' She gave him a contained little smile and walked without haste through the door he held open for her, and kept on walking up the stairs and along the gallery and into their bedroom, where at last she could give way to the grief which was too deep even for tears. For a long time she just lay face down on the bed, then, fearful Joss might come in and witness her misery, she got ready for the night, which was sleepless and lonely in the wide bed where she had known so much rapture during her brief marriage. Some time during the night she heard Joss in the room next door, bumping into the furniture as he got ready for bed. It sounded as though he, at least, had found solace in the whisky decanter. Perhaps she should have done the same. But later she heard him twisting and turning on the narrow couch next door, as far from sleep as she was, demonstrating that alcohol was no solution to their common predicament.

At breakfast next morning their estrangement was masked by the cheerful company of their son, whose foot was so much better that he could get about quite nimbly with the aid of a walking stick produced by the indefatigable Benson. To keep Tom off his foot as much as possible, Joss proposed a chess lesson during the morning, while Lucy kept out of the way, officially on the pretext of sorting out Tom's clothes to go back to school, but in reality with the aim of keeping her notoriously expressive face away from the searching gaze of her husband. The night had been unbearable. Again and again Lucy had been obliged to fight with herself to keep from running into the dressing-room to plead with Joss to come back where he belonged. From the shadows beneath his eyes she suspected he had fared little better. Tom cast a curious look at them both from time to time, as though suspicious something was wrong, but he refrained from comment, and ate an enormous lunch before getting ready to go back to school, leaving Lucy and Joss alone to finish their coffee as he hopped off to the kitchen to see the Bensons.

'You've eaten very little,' observed Joss.

'I wasn't hungry. In fact, I don't feel too good. I think I'm coming down with something.' It was the truth. Lucy's head was hot and aching and she felt sick, and knew very well she looked ghastly. Her Portuguese tan had faded to a wan shade of beige, and the shadows under her eyes were a match for her husband's.

He looked at her, frowning. 'If you don't feel well, go to bed and rest. I can drive Tom back to school on my own. I'm sure he won't mind.'

So was Lucy. Since Jonas Woodbridge's advent in Tom's life, it was plain his mother had to be content to take a back seat for a while. Which made it imperative for his parents to settle their differences, she decided. The thought of wrecking Tom's new-found happiness was unbearable.

'Thank you, Joss.' She gave him a grateful little smile. 'I do feel a bit seedy. Perhaps I can put in a bit of work on my accounts while you're away.'

Joss raised his eyesbrows. 'I hesitate to interfere,

Lucy, but I think a rest would be a better idea.' He turned, smiling, as Tom came back. 'Right then, young Tom. We'd better be off if we want to get you back in time for chapel. Your mother's going to stay behind, she's not feeling too grand.'

Tom was sympathetic, but obviously quite happy to go alone with Joss. To Lucy's amusement, he seemed more concerned with the enormous box of cakes and goodies supplied by Mrs Benson.

How quickly the young adapt, thought Lucy, as she waved them off later. Not so long ago I was the only mainstay in Tom's life. Now he has this place, security—and Joss. And I must see that he keeps them all, whatever I have to do to ensure it. She sighed, coughing drily as she went back in the house to see Mrs Benson.

'I'm going to lie down for a bit, Mrs B,' she said, putting her head round the kitchen door.

'Very sensible.' The housekeeper's eyes were anxious. 'You really don't look very well, Miss Lucy. Oh, dear, I must get into the habit of saying "Mrs Woodbridge".'

'Please don't,' begged Lucy and coughed again, dismayed by the sharp pain burning in her side.

Mrs Benson promptly marched Lucy up to her room and turned down the bed while she undressed. Lucy found it was quite wonderful to lie down. She was so tired suddenly that she wanted nothing more than blessed oblivion, to forget all the violent emotions churned up the night before. If only this nasty little pain would stop. Only it wasn't a little pain. It was a great big torment of a pain that clutched her ribs with a giant hand. It was a heart attack, thought Lucy in panic. She would never see Tom and Joss again. She should have begged Joss to sleep here in their bed with her last night. Perhaps they would never share this bed again. Oh, God! She wanted Joss here, now.

Mrs Benson, returning a few minutes later with a hot drink, took one look at Lucy's glittering eyes and burning cheeks and promptly rang the doctor.

'I don't need a doctor,' fretted Lucy, plucking at the quilt. 'I want Joss.'

'Yes, my lamb,' said Mrs Benson soothingly. 'He'll be back before long, you'll see.'

In actual fact, Joss returned while the doctor was with Lucy, and took the stairs in giant strides and burst into the bedroom.

'Lucy——' He looked in anguish at the man holding Lucy's wrist. 'Dr Manners—what is it? What's wrong with my wife?'

'Pleurisy, Mr Woodbridge.' The doctor laid Lucy's hand back on the quilt, and she tried to smile.

'Only pleurisy,' she croaked.

'Only!'

Dr Manners smiled as he closed his bag. 'Your wife thought she was having a heart attack.'

Joss gave every sign of following suit as he sat down abruptly on the edge of the bed and took Lucy's hand in his. 'The result of all those baked beans and brown bread, I suppose,' he said huskily.

Dr Manners looked mystified. 'On the contrary, a high-fibre diet is beneficial, Mr Woodbridge. Your wife's condition is probably the result of too much hard work and worry. Her constitution has decided to protest. Don't worry. She'll be all right in a few weeks or so.'

Lucy gasped, then coughed and clutched her side and Joss went white. 'But there's the shop,' she said, when she could speak.

Joss's response was short and excessively vulgar, and the doctor chuckled. 'Quite so, Mr Woodbridge. I'll leave you to sort that one out. In the meantime, I'll send round some medication for her.'

CHAPTER NINE

LUCY took longer than expected to recover. The illness was so untimely in every possible way that she worried about it constantly, impeding her recovery even as she strove so hard to achieve it.

'Lucy,' scolded Joss repeatedly, 'will you stop worrying yourself to death? Perdy's doing fine at the shop, Tom's in school, what do you have to fret about?'

Lucy couldn't bring herself to tell him. Her main preoccupation was her relationship with Joss, which was in an odd sort of abeyance due to a number of factors, not least of which was Dr Manners' blunt instructions that Lucy needed sleep, and plenty of it, undisturbed by any thoughts of an amatory nature for the time being. Which meant Joss continued to occupy his narrow couch in the dressing-room, while Lucy tossed and turned alone in their bed.

Their marriage picked its way through a minefield of things left unsaid, emotions instantly suppressed, of physical longings on Lucy's side that even the pleurisy failed to damp down after the first week or two. How Joss felt she had no idea. If he was prey to the same longings, he never exhibited them, taking refuge in finishing the book on Fiji. Shortly afterwards he went to London to visit his publishers and his agent, and looked troubled when he returned. Lucy was lying in a

garden chair on the lawn, feeling useless and
irritable because a little weeding had left her
washed out. Her face brightened at the sight of
Joss's tall, graceful figure. He took off the jacket
of his formal dark suit, and let himself down on the
grass with a sigh.

'What's the matter?' asked Lucy, after an
exchange of greetings. 'Something's obviously
wrong.'

'Lucy, how are you feeling? Truthfully?' Joss
looked at her searchingly.

'Much better. A bit tired if I do too much
weeding or whatever, but no more pain. Why?'

'I should leave for Brazil pretty soon, but I don't
like the idea of leaving you the way you are, all eyes
and——'

'Nose?' she put in, grinning.

'No.' He tapped the offending feature with a
gentle finger. 'I was about to say cheekbones.'

The thought of Joss's absence gave Lucy a
sharper pain than any the pleurisy had inflicted,
but she smiled to hide it, assuring him she was
perfectly well. 'As long as you can manage to fit in
Tom's cricket match before you go, there's really
no reason why you can't leave quite soon.'

Joss regarded her thoughtfully. 'If the
arrangements hadn't been set up well in advance I
wouldn't even contemplate it.'

'Of course you must go! When you get back I'll
be fit as a fiddle, I promise.'

Nevertheless, the effort of being bright and
cheerful during the days before Joss left took their
toll of Lucy's strength. She accompanied him to
Tom's school for the all-important cricket match,
and went out for a meal for the first time since their

return from Portugal, but he never made any move to share her bed, and when she had waved Joss off finally her utter loneliness without him was overwhelming.

'I think Dr Manners should take another look at you,' declared Mrs Benson, after Lucy's dinner tray went back to the kitchen that night almost untouched. 'He hasn't seen you for a week or two now, has he?'

Lucy wouldn't hear of a visit from the doctor. She would make an appointment in the usual way, then call in the shop to see how things were going under Perdy's management.

'Lord, you look seedy,' was that lady's reaction to her visitor. 'Sit down, for God's sake, and let me make you some tea.'

Lucy did as she was told, subsiding on the familiar chaise-longue so she could look round the shop while the kettle boiled. The place looked good. Perdy had asked to display some of her work, and a selection of exquisite plates and pots graced a credence table against one wall in the window, while farther back in the shop, where the light was less harmful, several watercolours of local scenery were grouped above one of Perdy's rare essays into the human form, the head of a young boy.

'You were going to let me buy that,' Lucy reminded her. 'Tom's unlikely to sit still long enough for me to commission another.'

'All right. I'll stick a "sold" sign on it.' Perdy handed her a cup of tea. 'I hope you don't mind, darling — I hung a few of Paul's pictures up.'

Lucy had no objection at all. The watercolours were very good; moody, atmospheric studies of copses of trees and inlets in river banks, very much to Lucy's taste. 'Paul's very talented,' she commented.

'Very—and, I might tell you, not only with a paintbrush. Oh, Lucy, you're blushing, and you an old married lady now.' Perdy hooted, then sobered. 'But tell me how you're feeling, love.'

'Astonished, I suppose. Dr Manners informs me I'm pregnant.' Lucy grinned at Perdy's startled expression. 'I was so wrapped up in my pleurisy, I never even gave it a thought. My general inertia merely means another Woodbridge is on the way.'

'Congratulations, love. Are you pleased?'

'Yes. I think so.'

'You don't sound terribly sure!'

'Well, it complicates things.' Lucy waved a hand about her. 'This place, for one.'

Perdy went over to the door and locked it, turning the 'Closed' sign outwards. 'Let's go into the office Lucy. I've a proposition to make.'

When Lucy returned to Abbot's Wood that evening she felt positively light-hearted. Her illness was no illness at all, but the promise of another son for Joss, and, what was more, Perdy and her Paul wanted to take over the shop, keeping it partly as it was, and partly as a gallery to display their own work.

Lucy wrote to Joss at length, at the box number he'd given her. She told him the news, reiterating her own pleasure at the prospect of the baby, making it crystal-clear she welcomed the thought of another child.

'This time, at least,' she wrote, 'he will come into the world in more conventional style. I'll let you know Tom's reaction when I write next.'

The Bensons were overjoyed at Lucy's news, and spoiled and fussed over her to such an extent she begged for mercy, and waited with anticipation for Joss's answer, since apart from a phone call when he arrived in Rio and a couple of brief notes afterwards en route for Amazonia, she hadn't heard from him. Tom, to Lucy's relief, was tickled pink at the idea of a new baby.

'Bannister *said* you would,' he reminded his mother. 'Will it be a boy, d'you think?'

Lucy made it clear that the choice of gender was not open to her, and Tom grinned and said he'd try to like it if it was a girl, but he'd rather have a boy if she could manage it. Joss's views on the subject were still unknown, as in his most recent letter he had written that none of hers had caught up with him yet. His anxiety for her health was apparent in every line, and Lucy worried over him, missing him badly, and repeated her news in every letter in case her others had gone astray.

While her pregnancy was still reasonably unnoticeable Lucy took Tom away to Cornwall for a couple of weeks during the summer holidays, and enjoyed the novelty and luxury of a hotel instead of their usual self-catering cottage. Tom enjoyed it too, but was a little wistful Joss couldn't have been with them.

'We'll all go somewhere together when he comes home,' Lucy assured him, but as the holidays wore on she worried about the absence of any letters from Joss while she was away. She rang the Bensons every night, but there had been no mail from Brazil. In some ways she was glad to return to Abbot's Wood. Illogically, she felt nearer to Joss there. But the moment she caught sight of Benson at the station cold fear gripped Lucy's heart. Tom helped her down from the train with great care as Benson came to take their luggage.

'Hello, Benson, what's up?' he asked bluntly.

'Welcome home, Miss Lucy, Mr Tom.' Benson hesitated and hefted two of the cases, leaving Tom to carry his own. 'Shall we get in the car first?'

First. Lucy's heart sank and she swallowed as she felt an unmistakable flutter in the region of her midriff. Baby Woodbridge was making his presence felt.

'What is it, Benson?' she asked urgently, once they were in the car.

'Mr Joss's agent, Mr Shelton, has been in touch, Miss Lucy. It seems the light plane Mr Joss was travelling in hasn't been heard of. The British Embassy in Rio conveyed the message, and will inform you as soon as any further details are known.

Tom looked sick, but his hand clasped Lucy's firmly. 'Don't worry, Mother. Joss will be OK. He's probably crash-landed somewhere. By now I expect he's fighting his way through the jungle.'

Somehow, Lucy managed to smile. She had no heart to say Joss wasn't Superman. As far as Tom was concerned he was. 'I'm sure you're right,' she agreed, her voice surprising her with its steadiness. 'Maybe there'll be more news by the time we get home.'

Both Lewis Shelton and an official from the Embassy rang her that evening, but only to confirm what Lucy already knew. As soon as there was any news she would be informed, she was told with sympathy.

'If there's anything I can do, Lucy,' said Lewis Shelton with feeling, 'just say the word.'

Lucy thanked him, but there was nothing anyone could do, except Joss. And he was lost somewhere in the dense jungle of the Amazon basin. But only lost. Lucy held on to that tightly, never for a moment allowing herself to think of him as lost to her for ever.

Tom stayed very close to Lucy that evening, huddled against her on the leather chesterfield as though her proximity was comforting. Lucy was glad. She, too, needed the simple contact of her son's hand on hers, and it was with reluctance that she finally sent him off to bed. Mrs Benson, her face lined with worry, insisted Lucy drink some hot milk to help her sleep, and Lucy downed it to please her, though she doubted sleep was likely, that night or any other, until she knew Joss was safe.

The days dragged by. No further news came. Tom was afraid to leave Lucy's side at first, sure the phone would ring at any moment. When it did, it was usually Joss's agent or his editor, both of them assuring her everything possible was being done to find her husband, that Brazilian pilots were among the best in the world, and that he was certain to be found. Lucy listened and thanked them, assured them that she was perfectly all right, and never gave utterance to the words screaming in her brain, that she wanted Joss back, and why wasn't everyone moving heaven and earth to find him?

After a while Tom resumed his old practice of fishing with Ben Todd, who all but lived at Abbot's Wood in the time before school was due to start.

Lucy was grateful for his presence, which meant
she could be on her own now and then, and give
way a little, as she dared not when Tom was
around. Her condition grew more visible by the
day. The baby had been shy of making its presence
known in the beginning, but was making up for it
now at a great rate, a fact commented on by Perdy,
who came to visit almost daily once she had shut up
shop.

'Joss will turn up,' she said firmly.

Lucy nodded. 'If I didn't truly believe that I'd go
mad.' She patted her stomach. 'And that wouldn't
do young Woodbridge any good at all, would it?'

By dishing out reassurance to Tom and the
Bensons, Lucy found she gained some herself,
managing to get through each day by the simple
expedient of telling herself that Joss was alive
somewhere. If he was dead, she would know. It
was this certainty alone which kept her in one piece
as time passed with no news of Joss, and all too
soon it was time for Tom to return to school. Lucy
was glad for him. He would be better fully occuped
in the company of his friends than trying so
manfully to be a prop and mainstay to his mother.

To her surprise, Lucy felt very well in the second
half of her pregnancy, despite her constant state of
mental anguish. Doggedly she ate and drank the
things Dr Manners recommended, exercised and
gardened, and helped Mrs Benson in the house.
She knitted and read and had dinner with Perdy
and Paul, and went regularly to church, even
though it meant running the gauntlet of
Abbotsbridge's sympathetic enquiries. She prayed
for Joss's safe return every night, but derived
additional comfort from the ritual of the church

service every Sunday.

Autumn was particularly beautiful that year it seemed to Lucy, as Tom came home for half-term and went back again, but the November day was grey with mist when she received the news. The light aircraft Joss had been travelling in had been located, and a body recovered from the wreckage. After weeks in the jungle identification was difficult, but the body was believed to be that of her husband.

Lucy put down the telephone in a daze, and turned to see the Bensons hovering, their faces mirroring the pain in hers. Her brain refused to accept the fact that Joss was dead, yet he must be because pain was clutching at her at the very thought. She gasped, and Mrs Benson took her in her arms, rocking her gently, crooning comfort even as she wept herself.

'It's not true!' cried Lucy in anguish. 'It can't be. I love him so much . . .' She gave a smothered cry as the pain tore at her again.

'What is it?' cried Mrs Benson, alarmed.

'I'm afraid it's the baby!'

Pandemonium reigned while the weeping housekeeper ran to pack. Benson rang the hospital, and in no time Lucy was lying on the delivery table in the maternity ward, coming to terms with the fact that her child was determined to make his entry into the world much too early. She struggled to do as she was told, but her body and her baby were bent on doing their own thing, and it was agony and endless until at last she screamed for Joss and it was over.

'Is he all right?' she gasped, terrified.

'He'll have to put up with life in an incubator for

a while because he's a bit small.' The staff nurse smiled down at her reassuringly. 'But he's all in one piece, except for one important bit, Mrs Woodbridge. He's a she!'

Lucy stared up at the young woman in tearful wonder.

'Will Daddy be disappointed?' asked the nurse.

The tears rolled down Lucy's cheeks. 'No. He—he——' Great sobs began to shake her, and at once Lucy was given something to make her sleep at last, to give her relief from all the pain in mind and body of the past few hours.

Tom was allowed home the weekend Lucy brought her daughter from the hospital. In spite of her premature arrival in the world, little Miss Woodbridge had needed only a short time in an incubator before she was pronounced fit to go home.

'Gosh, she's small,' said a subdued Tom as a minuscule fist closed round his little finger. '*And* she's noisy,' he added, as his sister demanded sustenance.

'Very true,' agreed Lucy, and shut her daughter up by putting a bottle in her mouth. 'Are you all right, Tom?'

He nodded listlessly. 'I'm OK.' His slate-blue eyes met hers, and Lucy felt a wrenching at her heart. 'Maybe it was a mistake, Mother. Maybe it wasn't Joss.'

Lucy swallowed hard. He was only saying what she felt herself, but it was cruel to foster any false hope in Tom's heart. 'I think we'll have to get used to the idea, Tom. I'm afraid it's just you and me again, only this time we've got this little bundle to look after.'

'And the Bensons,' said Tom, obviously trying to give comfort. 'And we live here now. You don't have to work, I mean.'

'No, darling. So we just have to make the best of things. Joss——' she faltered a moment, then went on. 'Joss wouldn't like us to be miserable.'

Tom nodded, too full up to speak for a moment, then sniffed hard. 'I just wish Joss could have had *one* Christmas with us, though.'

Tom's cry from the heart echoed in Lucy's mind over and over again in the time before the festive season. Festive season, she thought with derision. It would be anything but that. Nevertheless, for Tom's sake, and even for the sake of the demanding little scrap of humanity that kept her awake at nights, she would just have to try to make Christmas as happy as possible. It would be hard. God knew, there was nothing she wanted in the shape of a gift other than Joss in her arms again. Lucy blocked her mind to the thought. That way lay anguish, she knew. She would just have to resign herself to life without Joss. And to cursing herself continually for wasting ten years of their lives when they could have been together.

Lucy's daughter thrived steadily, and was beginning to give her mother more rest at night by the time Tom came home for Christmas. Her son was more sober than usual, but seemed to have adjusted to his grief very well, Lucy found, and to her great relief he seemed utterly taken with his small sister.

'You still looked tired,' he commented, when he greeted Lucy. 'Does the baby keep you awake a lot?'

'Not so much now.' Lucy smiled. 'I never got round to apologising for not producing a brother for you, by the way.'

He chuckled. 'I don't mind. Besides,' he added, 'it's not your fault.'

Lucy thanked him drily. 'Big of you to admit it.'

'It was Joss's fault, actually.'

Lucy spluttered over the cup of tea she was drinking. 'It's not anyone's *fault*, Tom.'

'No, I know. I mean, it's the man who determines the sex of a child,' Tom informed her kindly.

Christmas came with relentless speed, but in some ways Lucy was grateful to it. Due to the rush of shopping and preparations for the Christmas dinner Perdy and Paul were coming to share with them, plus the demands of her daughter, she was so tired that she slept a little better than usual. Added to which, it was such a comfort to have Tom at home. She got up early on Christmas Eve to bathe and feed the baby so that she and Tom could have breakfast in peace while the Bensons kept an eye on the tiny autocrat who ruled Abbot's Wood these days.

While they ate, Tom ticked off the various items of importance that had been dealt with to his satisfaction.

'Tree's up, presents are packed—did you remember the baby's Christmas stocking?'

Lucy assured him nothing had been overlooked. As far as she was concerned, everything had been done. 'Today I intend to have as much of a rest as young miss will allow me before helping prepare for the meal tomorrow. I can't leave everything to Mrs Benson.'

Tom went off to make sure the Bensons were coping with his sister, while Lucy took advantage of the respite to enjoy a second cup of coffee. She became engrossed in the morning paper, hardly noticing when the doorbell rang, assuming it was the postman. She turned, unsuspecting, as the door opened some time later, expecting Tom with another sheaf of Christmas cards, then began to shake uncontrollably, her eyes starting from her head. The figure in the doorway was in dire need of a haircut, his clothes shabby and ill-fitting, his eyes bloodshot and tired in his haggard face, but it was nevertheless Joss, and Lucy gave a hoarse cry, tears pouring down her face as she hurled herself across the room into his outstretched arms and buried her face against his chest, holding him so tight she could feel his heart thudding against hers. She threw her head back and smiled incandescently into Joss's eyes, and his mouth met hers and life was worth living once more.

'Did you get my message?' he muttered against her lips.

'What message?' She kissed him hard, not interested in messages. Joss was here in her arms, and that was all she needed to know.

'Someone was supposed to contact you yesterday,' he said huskily, then kissed her again, hungrily, his hands running up and down her back, holding her close, and Lucy freed her mouth unwillingly.

'Something was wrong with the line.'

'It still is—I tried to ring from the station.' Joss didn't wait for her answer, and Lucy found that kissing him was so much more vital to her well-being than words that she responded fiercely, wanting him to know how much she'd missed him and wanted him right here in her arms like this.

'They said you were dead,' she said at one point.

'I'm not. I'm very much alive.' Joss took her face in his hands. 'I had no intention of making you a widow before you'd even got used to being my wife. Are you better, my darling?'

Better? Lucy grinned at him with such mischief, Joss crushed her in his arms again. 'Oh yes, I'm better, Joss Woodbridge, but I had to get a lot worse before I managed a complete recovery.' Her smiled died. 'What happened, Joss?'

'We crashed, we walked,' he said simply. 'The other passenger in the plane was killed, but the pilot and I survived. I finally got to my Indians on foot. We lived with them until we were found.'

'As simple as that?' Lucy touched his face with loving fingers. 'You're thin. And lined.'

'And ugly, by the sound of it.' He caught her fingers and kissed them.

'You're the most beautiful man in the world,' said Lucy, and watched in awe as a great tide of colour rose in Joss's face, then closed her eyes, trembling, as he began to kiss her with a sense of purpose she recognised. She responded gladly, until a knock on the door interrupted them and Joss swung round, holding her in the crook of his arm as Tom said diffidently, 'Hi, Dad. Can we come in?'

'Tom!' In a couple of strides, Joss was across the room to hug his son, stopping short in astonishment as he realised Tom was carrying a small bundle with great care. 'Good lord! What's this?'

Tom glanced at his mother for guidance, then at

her nod he grinned. 'Not "what". "Who". This is Miss Olivia Woodbridge,' he announced with ceremony, then tickled the baby under her chin. 'Liv, wake up. This is your dad.'

Joss stared wildly at the baby Tom thrust into his arms, his eyes incredulous as he looked from the baby to Lucy.

'She's a bit premature, and she's not a boy,' Lucy said with apology, 'but she's got all the right bits and pieces——'

'Especially a voice,' said Tom with feeling. 'She's been kicking up a terrible racket in the kitchen—didn't you hear her?'

'Well, no,' admitted Joss, still fascinated by his daughter. 'I was too busy kissing your mother.'

Tom nodded matter-of-factly. 'Thought you might be, so I kept out of the way for a bit. Mrs Benson said it's time for her feed, by the way.'

And right on cue Olivia Woodbridge opened her mouth in corroboration.

'Good lord,' said Joss in a panic, looking so helpless that both Tom and Lucy laughed outright. 'Don't just stand there! *Do* something.'

'I expect you'd like to be alone with Mother now,' said Tom kindly. 'Will you tell me everything about what happened after the baby's been fed?'

Joss's face softened, and with great care he handed the squalling baby to Lucy before putting an arm round Tom's shoulders and squeezing hard. 'You bet I will. Sorry to be so dumbfounded, son, but the surprise packet you gave me rather took the wind out of my sails.' He gave Tom a hug, then eyed the table. 'Tell you what, Tom. Ask Mrs Benson to cook me some wonderful British bacon and eggs, and I'll eat them while this noisy sister of yours has her breakfast.'

Tom ran off with alacrity and Joss put an arm round Lucy, hanging over their daughter in awe.

'God, darling, she's a miracle,' he breathed, his cheek rubbing over Lucy's hair.

'She's also the reason I didn't recover from my pleurisy very quickly. Oh, Joss, I was so thrilled to be pregnant, but so unhappy that I couldn't share my joy with you.' And to her annoyance Lucy's eyes filled with tears that rolled down her cheeks on to the baby's face, and Joss bent to kiss them away, holding her close.

'Don't cry, darling, you're tearing me apart. I swear I'll never leave you again for longer than five minutes if I can help it.' He laughed shakily. 'Just look what you get up to when my back's turned!'

'You never received even *one* of my letters, then?'

'No. They're probably in a great bundle somewhere. I didn't try to trace them; I just wanted to get home, so I got on the first plane I could. I suppose I should have rung from Rio——' Joss paused and Lucy looked at him questioningly. 'Well, things were a bit uncertain between us when I left,' he went on. 'I was human enough to want to surprise you, gauge your reaction before you could hide it.'

'Oh, were you? And are you satisfied?' she demanded.

His eyes kindled. 'The look in your eyes just now was something I'll dream about for the rest of my life.' His arm tightened about her possessively and he kissed her mouth for a fierce moment, until Olivia Woodbridge let out a howl of protest and her parents laughed shakily, neither of them far from tears at the wonder of their reunion.

Then Mrs Benson arrived with much-needed sustenance for them all, and, as Joss relieved her of a tray laden with everything a man could desire for breakfast, life was suddenly wonderfully normal. Joss ate hugely and related the gist of his adventures, and Lucy told how she'd sold her stock to Perdy, who now leased Abbotsbridge Antiques in partnership with Paul. Then there was much laughter as Joss tried his hand at changing a nappy, and finally the baby was left with Mrs Benson while Lucy, Joss and Tom settled in front of a roaring fire in the study to go into the tale of Joss's adventures in more detail. Tom was deeply impressed.

'What was the worst bit?' he asked.

Joss looked at Lucy as he answered. 'Just before the plane crashed, I thought I might never see my wife and son again. After we were down, and survival was up to my own resources I felt sure I could make it. The man who died was unfortunate enough to fracture his skull, we thought, at the moment of impact, but the pilot and I were extraordinarily lucky, because apart from a few bruises neither of us was injured. We were starving by the time we reached the Arani, and off our heads with fever, but the Arani doctored us and fed us, and we survived our fever and their medicine, and I'm here to tell the tale.'

Lucy shuddered. 'Could you keep to more ordinary trips in future, Joss, please?'

His eyes were grave as he looked from her to Tom. 'No more wandering for me, Lucy. From now on I'll stay home and have a shot at writing fiction.'

'Which can hardly be stranger than truth in our case.'

'That's for sure,' said Tom in such a heartfelt tone his parents looked at him in surprise. He flushed to the roots of his curly, dark hair. 'I—I heard you both talking that night,' he said in a choked voice.

Joss exchanged a startled look with Lucy, then sat down on the sofa by Tom. 'Which night?' he asked gently.

'When I cut my foot.' Tom looked hunted, and chewed the tip of his finger. 'I got thirsty, so I hopped down the stairs. I got to the study door and heard you and Mother talking about—blood groups.'

Lucy went pale. 'Did you hear it all?'

Tom shook his head violently. 'Just the bit about Joss being my father not—not Simon, then I scooted back to bed.'

Joss put an arm round his son's shoulders. 'And how did you feel about that?'

'Great,' said Tom simply, then frowned. 'Would you have married Mother right at the start if she'd told you?' he added anxiously.

Joss directed a look at his wife that melted her bones. 'I always wanted to marry your mother, Tom.'

'Likewise,' she said demurely, her dark eyes bright with love as she smiled back.

'Will I be Tom Woodbridge now?' asked her son.'

'Do you want to be?' asked Joss.

Tom looked torn. 'The thing is, would Gramp mind, d'you think?'

'He'd be delighted,' said Lucy with certainty. 'Your grandfather thought I was very unkind to Joss.'

'So did Joss,' murmured her husband, and Tom grinned.

'OK, then,' he said, jumping up. 'It'll be easier when I go to the new school, anyway. Shall I go and get the baby?'

'By all means.' Lucy smiled at him lovingly. 'Wheel her in and give poor Mrs Benson some peace.'

Peace, however, proved elusive in the Woodbridge house for the rest of the day, since the outer world, in the shape of the media, had got wind of Joss's return and the house was beseiged by reporters and cameras. Tom was cock-a-hoop to see himself on the television newscast that evening as part of a Christmas story that touched the nation's hearts. Lucy and Joss called the Bensons in to watch with them as the tall, gauntly handsome man and his radiant wife and son faced the cameras, the latter proudly carrying a small, squalling bundle.

'A human fairy story,' said the attractive lady newsreader, smiling at the camera, 'with a real-life happy ending.'

'Amen to that,' said Joss, as he sat with one arm round Lucy, the other round Tom. Both the Bensons were frankly wet-eyed, and it needed a round of celebration drinks for all concerned before more mundane thoughts could be turned to dinner.

'This is the happiest night of my life,' said Lucy, when she and Joss were finally alone in their room. He smiled at her and held her close, his hand gentle as he stroked her curls. 'Mine, too. God, how I've longed for this moment, darling.'

She tipped her head back to look at him. 'You mean with Tom and Olivia asleep and time to ourselves at last?' To her surprise, Joss shook his head.

'To hear you say what you just said, Lucy Woodbridge, I would have crawled through the jungle to Manaus on my hands and knees.'

At the look in his eyes, her smile faded and she buried her face against his shoulder. 'Oh, Joss, if you knew how I've hated myself these past endless months——'

'Hated? Why?'

'Because of all the wasted years when we could have been together!' She burrowed closer against him, her arms clutching him painfully tight as she felt his ribs. 'I tried to keep faith with my certainty that you were alive. I felt all along, you see, that I would have known if you were dead. I just couldn't believe that our life together was over. But some days I felt low, and then I'd brood over the time we *could* have had together, and I'd lash out at myself.' She threw her head back, her eyes brilliant with sincerity as they met his. 'But you see, Joss, it never occurred to me that you could have cared for me. You were such a god to me, a deity on the heights of Olympus. I never in my wildest dreams imagined you spared a thought for Lucy Drummond.'

Joss shook her gently, then brought his mouth down on hers and kissed her until they were both shaking. He pressed her face against his chest, rubbing his cheek against her hair. 'I'm no god, Lucy. I'm mortal. Very mortal. In fact, right at this moment, the base human male in me is threatening to get out of hand. I've longed for you so much, sweetheart.'

Lucy's response was fierce for a moment, then she pulled away, but only to take her husband by the hand and lead him to the bed. She paused as the bells rang out on the still night air, and smiled with joy into Joss's face. 'Merry Christmas, darling!'

He picked her up and stood with her in his arms, smiling down into her radiant face. 'I'm afraid I didn't manage any Christmas shopping in my hurry to get home to you, Lucy.'

'You've brought me the thing I want most in the world,' she assured him passionately. 'You came back to me. As a gift, that makes all others pale into insignificance.'

Six months later, on a sunlit evening in June, Lucy Woodbridge sat enthralled in front of a television programme entitled *Miracle in the Jungle*. Told by Joss with great simplicity, the story of survival and endurance and ultimate rescue was extraordinarily moving. Although the cameraman had so tragically died in the crash, one of his cameras survived, and Joss's commentary was accompanied by his own amateur photography. Lucy watched, her throat constricting, as Joss spoke over shots of the rain-forest as they fought their way through it. His words were undramatic but descriptive, and vividly communicated the claustrophobic density of the jungle, with its towering canopy of trees, and lush, green undergrowth. She could almost hear the hum of swarming insect life, the screech of monkeys, feel the humid heat. There were shots of the shy, primitive Arani, and their *malocas*, the lodges raised on stilts, where entire families lived under one palm-thatched roof in their clearing at the edge of the Amazon, but only one glimpse of Joss, filmed by the Brazilian pilot, and Lucy sniffed hard as she saw the gaunt, bearded face.

'Don't cry, darling,' said Joss, watching her.

'I'm not crying—hush!' Lucy remained riveted to the screen until the credits appeared at the end and she sat back with a sigh. 'God, Joss, you were so lucky!'

'I know.' He reached over and pulled her on to his lap. 'I must be the luckiest man in the world. I've got you and Tom and little Miss Surprise Packet up there in bed.'

Lucy wriggled against him contentedly. 'Did she go down peacefully?'

'No. I left her protesting, but since she's had her supper and I'd played with her for a while I left her to it. If we didn't watch it, that young lady would rule us all, Tom included.' Joss ran his lips over Lucy's cheek. 'I told her very firmly I wanted some peace and quiet with her mother.'

Lucy held him tight. 'Amen to that. Do you suppose I'll ever get over wanting to clutch at you, make sure you're there all the time?'

'I hope not—I like it so much.' Joss chuckled and kissed her. 'Lucy Woodbridge, have you any idea how much I love you?'

She pretended to think it over. 'As much as I love you, perhaps?'

'More!'

'Impossible!'

Joss kissed her again, then settled her with her head tucked into his shoulder. 'I thought we might

go back to Portugal this summer, darling. Take
Tom and Liv, and see if Senhora Vargas will let us
have the house again. Plus the maid whose services
I refused last time.'

Lucy's head came up. 'You never mentioned any
maid when we were there, Joss Woodbridge!'

'For obvious reasons, I wanted complete
privacy.' Joss kissed her nose. 'I didn't want
someone coming in to sweep the bedroom floor at
inopportune moments.'

'And to think I did all that cooking and
bedmaking——'

'Not *that* much.'

'True.' Lucy smiled at him happily. 'I think it's a
great idea, only Tom might find it a bit boring,
don't you think?'

'Tell him to bring his pal—Bannister, is it? Or
young Ben Todd from the village. Throw in some
fishing tackle and I think Tom will jump at the
idea.'

'You're right. You make a very good father,
Joss, considering how recently you've taken on the
job.'

His eyes glinted under lowered lids. 'And how do
I shape up as a husband?'

'Very nicely,' Lucy said primly, then gasped as
Joss undid the zip of her dress and slid it fron her
shoulders. As his lips began a leisurely exploration
she shivered and made a token protest. 'Joss—it's
broad daylight.'

'What has that to do with anything?' But Joss
sat up obediently, and zipped up her dress.

Lucy tried to hide her disappointment. Joss
wasn't normally so easy to tame.

'Want to hear my next idea?' he asked, grinning.

'I'm sure you're going to tell me anyway!'

'True.' Joss's face took on an expression Lucy viewed with suspicion. 'It's Sunday,' he said. 'The Bensons won't be back until morning, young Olivia is quiet for the moment, so I thought we might get an early night. Unless you want to watch the Hitchcock film on the box.'

'I've seen it. Twice.' Lucy shrugged. 'So if you're tired——'

'No. Quite the reverse.' Joss stood up and stretched, looked tanned and rested and utterly irresistible to his wife. 'But I might point out, my lovely lady, that there are ten years of my life you have to make up to me. And since my little sojourn in the Brazilian rain-forest I'm fired with the urge to make the most of every minute of the rest of my life with you. This doesn't mean I need to be making love to you *all* the time, you understand. I like just being with you, whatever we're doing. But now, right at this moment, I want to take you up to bed and make love to you at great length, savouring every second, until we both fall asleep, too exhausted to do anything else.'

Lucy's eyes danced as she jumped to her feet. 'That's even more attractive a programme than the one I've just watched, Joss Woodbridge!'

Some time later, when the house was dark and quiet, Joss smoothed his wife's tangled curls away from her damp forehead and gave a great sigh of utter content. 'Did you ever imagine, my darling, during all those years of hating me, that we would ever be together like this?'

'No,' said Lucy with dry emphasis. 'My imagination was nowhere near vivid enough.'

'That wasn't what I meant,' said Joss

reprovingly. 'Not the sex part—wonderful though it is. I meant you, me, Tom, the baby. Sometimes I can't believe it's all real.'

Lucy bit his shoulder gently. 'Just to prove we're not dreaming.'

'Ouch!' Joss was quiet for a while. 'Lucy, will you be angry if I asked a very personal question?'

'I won't know until you ask it!'

'On our honeymoon, you were very nervous for a lady of some twenty-eight summers and mother of a ten-year-old son. If I hadn't known otherwise, I could have sworn it was the first time for you.'

'So ham-fisted, you mean!'

Joss laughed and held her close. 'No. So full of wonder, I think I mean.'

'That was because you're such a wonderful lover, Joss Woodbridge. And don't tell me you haven't been told that thousands of times, because I won't believe you.'

'Hundreds,' he corrected modestly.

Lucy giggled, then fell silent. 'I suppose I might as well confess,' she said after a while. 'Our honeymoon wasn't the first time a man had made love to me, as you would know better than anyone. But it was the second.' She felt Joss's body tense against hers.

'You mean, there's never been anyone else?' He sat up and switched on the light so he could see her face. 'Only me, Lucy?'

'Got it in one. Only you. First love, last love, hero, villain, you've always been a one-man show in my life, Joss Woodbridge. You were a hard act to follow.' Lucy sighed. 'To be perfectly honest, I first got to know Simon just so I could be in your vicinity. Funny, isn't it? Jonas Woodbridge, the

handsomest man in the county, and little Lucy
Drummond. How my friends would have laughed.
Not that I wasn't fond of Simon, believe me. I
loved him too, in a different way—in fact, those
same friends all thought he was the one I was nutty
over. Not a soul ever suspected I was agonising
over you all the time.'

'Least of all me!' Joss looked at her in awe.
'Dear God, Lucy——'

'Which,' she interrupted fiercely, 'is how you
came to make love to me that day. I wanted you to
more than anything else in the world—so much
that nothing and no one else mattered, not even
Simon. And certainly not Caroline,' she added
with candour.

'Do you regret it, my darling?' Joss's voice was
deeply tender.

'How could I,' she said simply, 'when Tom was
the result? And now you and I are together and we
have Liv as well, after our years in the wilderness.
It's a long time since I thought of you as a villain,
Joss.'

A flame lit in Joss's eyes. 'Am I allowed to know
exactly how you *do* think of me, Lucy?'

'Shall I throw my arms round your neck and
murmur "my hero" in throbbing tones?' she
teased.

Joss shook his head and put the light out. 'Just
love me, Lucy.'

'I do. I always will.'

'I need convincing. I think you should *show* me
how much—right now.'

Lucy laughed breathlessly. 'I would, willingly,
but I think I just heard the voice of the turtle.'

Joss held her prisoner. 'If you mean our demanding daughter, she'll just have to wait while I teach her mother a lesson in priorities.'

'I don't need lessons. *You* are my first priority, believe me, now and always. Oh, Joss . . .'

In the next room, Miss Olivia Woodbridge gave another tentative wail. She waited expectantly, then wailed again. When no one came, she grumbled desultorily, then thrust a thumb in her mouth. She sucked drowsily for a while, then eventually went back to sleep, leaving her parents to pursue, undisturbed, the path to their own private paradise.

Harlequin Presents

Coming Next Month

Available in April wherever paperback books are sold, or through Harlequin Reader Service:

In the U.S.
901 Fuhrmann Blvd.
P.O. Box 1397
Buffalo, N.Y. 14240-1397

In Canada
P.O. Box 603
Fort Erie, Ontario
L2A 5X3

Harlequin Regency Romance™

Romance the way it was *always* meant to be!

The time is 1811, when a Regent Prince rules the empire. The place is London, the glittering capital where rakish dukes and dazzling debutantes scheme and flirt in a dangerously exciting game. Where marriage is the passport to wealth and power, yet every girl hopes secretly for love....

Welcome to Harlequin Regency Romance where reading is an adventure and romance is *not* just a thing of the past! Two delightful books a month, beginning May '89.

Available wherever Harlequin Books are sold.

◈ *Harlequin Superromance*

**Here are the longer, more involving stories you
have been waiting for...Superromance.**

Modern, believable novels of love, full of the complex
joys and heartaches of real people.

Intriguing conflicts based on today's constantly
changing life-styles.

Four new titles every month.
Available wherever paperbacks are sold.

COMING IN MARCH FROM

Harlequin Superromance

Book Two of the Merriman County Trilogy
AFTER ALL THESE YEARS
the sizzle of Eve Gladstone's
One Hot Summer continues!

Sarah Crewes is at it again, throwing Merriman County into a tailspin with her archival diggings. In *One Hot Summer* (September 1988) she discovered that the town of Ramsey Falls was celebrating its tricentennial one year too early.

Now she's found that Riveredge, the Creweses' ancestral home and property, does not rightfully belong to her family. Worse, the legitimate heir to Riveredge may be none other than the disquieting Australian, Tyler Lassiter.

Sarah's not sure why Tyler's in town, but she suspects he is out to right some old wrongs—and some new ones!

The unforgettable characters of *One Hot Summer* and *After All These Years* will continue to delight you in book three of the trilogy. Watch for *Wouldn't It Be Lovely* in November 1989.

SR349-1